Gertrude Chandler Warner's

THE BOXCAR CHILDREN

GRAPHIC NOVELS

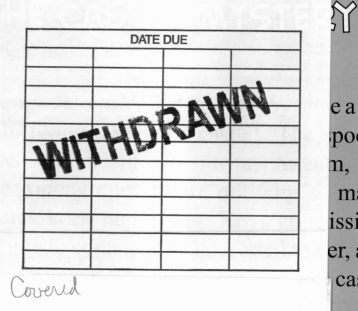
T   MYSTERY

H   e a fun
new jo   spooky
old pla   m, but
first th   many
odd th   issing,
strange   er, and
soon t   castle
has an

THE BOXCAR CHILDREN
GRAPHIC NOVELS

THE BOXCAR CHILDREN

SURPRISE ISLAND

THE YELLOW HOUSE MYSTERY

MYSTERY RANCH

MIKE'S MYSTERY

BLUE BAY MYSTERY

SNOWBOUND MYSTERY

TREE HOUSE MYSTERY

THE HAUNTED CABIN MYSTERY

THE AMUSEMENT PARK MYSTERY

THE PIZZA MYSTERY

THE CASTLE MYSTERY

Gertrude Chandler Warner's

THE BOXCAR CHILDREN
THE CASTLE MYSTERY

Adapted by Shannon Eric Denton
Illustrated by Mike Dubisch

Henry Alden

Watch

Jessie Alden

Violet Alden

Benny Alden

Visit us at www.albertwhitman.com.

Copyright © 2010 by Abdo Consulting Group, Inc. All rights reserved. Published
in 2010 by Albert Whitman & Company by arrangement with Abdo Consulting
Group, Inc. No part of this book may be reproduced in any form without written
permission from the publisher. THE BOXCAR CHILDREN® is a registered
trademark of Albert Whitman & Company.

Adapted by Shannon Eric Denton
Illustrated by Mike Dubisch
Colored by Wes Hartman
Lettered by Johnny Lowe
Edited by Stephanie Hedlund
Interior layout and design by Kristen Fitzner Denton
Cover art by Mike Dubisch
Book design and packaging by Shannon Eric Denton

Library of Congress Cataloging-in-Publication Data
is available from the Library of Congress.

10 9 8 7 6 5 4 3 2 1 LB 14 13 12 11 10 09

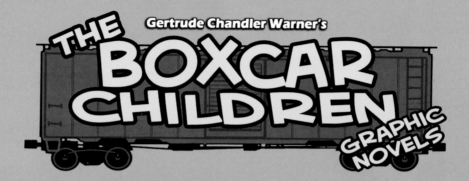

Gertrude Chandler Warner's

THE BOXCAR CHILDREN GRAPHIC NOVELS

THE CASTLE MYSTERY

Contents

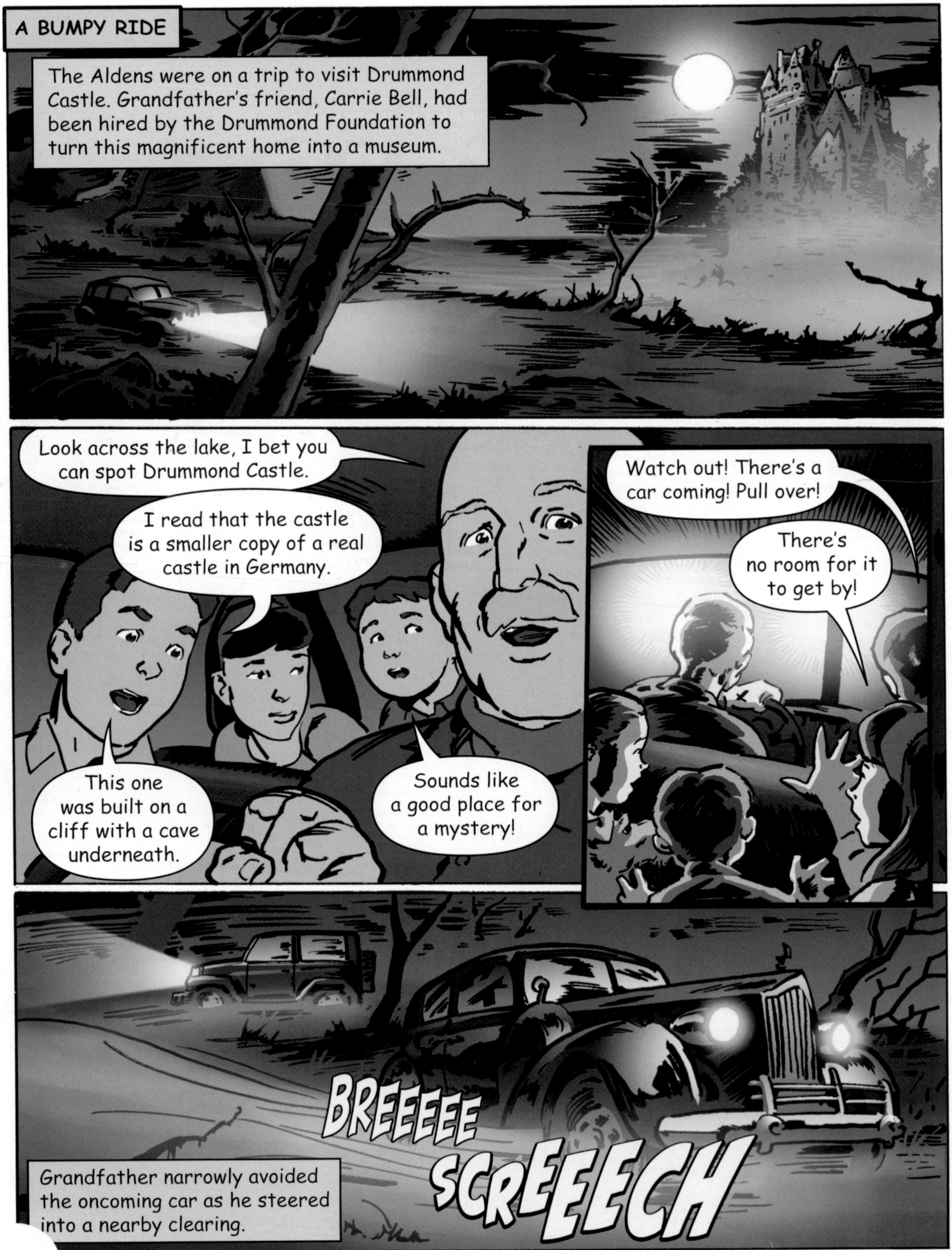
A BUMPY RIDE
The Aldens were on a trip to visit Drummond Castle. Grandfather's friend, Carrie Bell, had been hired by the Drummond Foundation to turn this magnificent home into a museum.
Look across the lake, I bet you can spot Drummond Castle.
I read that the castle is a smaller copy of a real castle in Germany.
This one was built on a cliff with a cave underneath.
Sounds like a good place for a mystery!
Watch out! There's a car coming! Pull over!
There's no room for it to get by!
BREEEEE
SCREEEECH
Grandfather narrowly avoided the oncoming car as he steered into a nearby clearing.

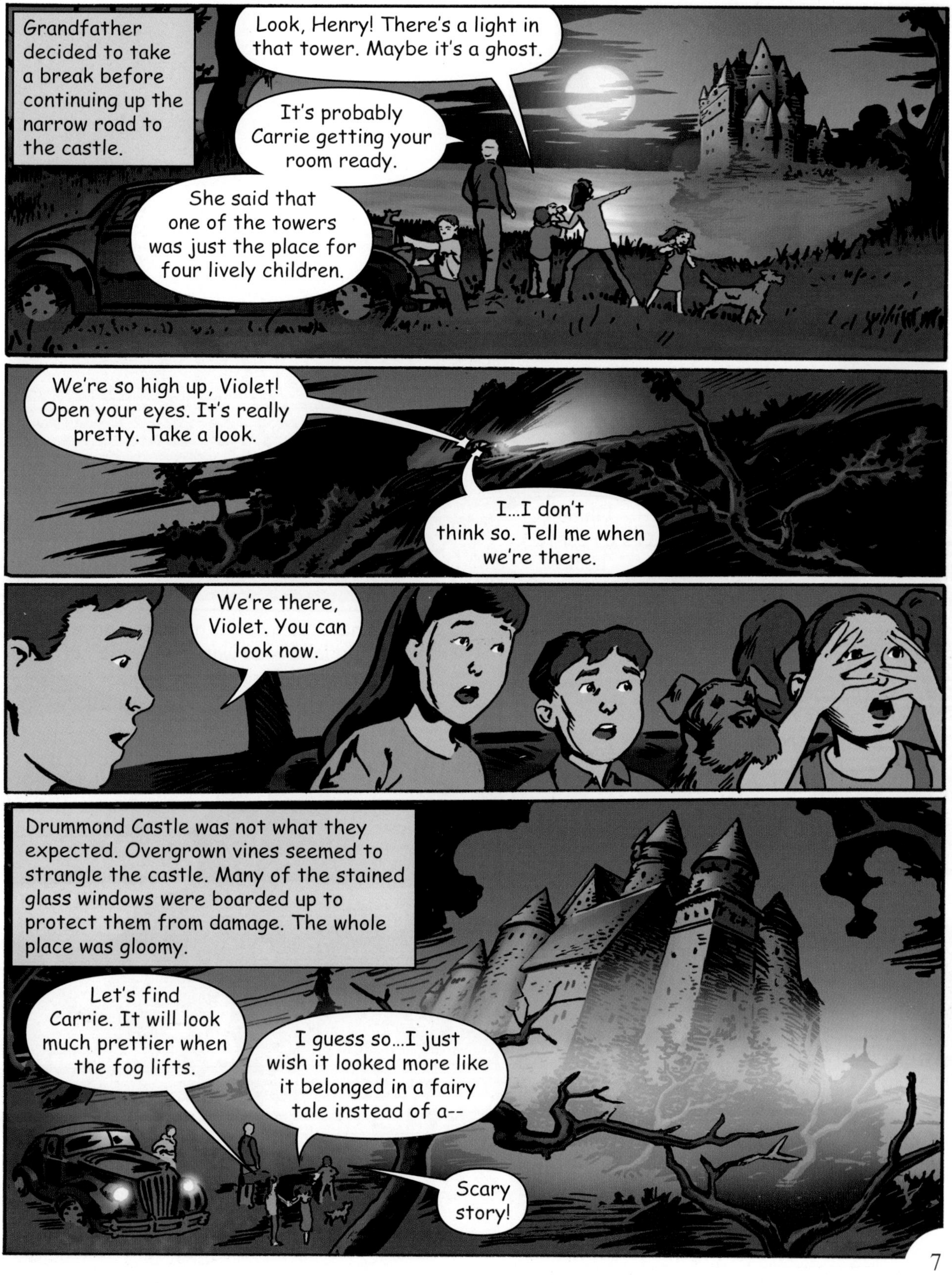

Grandfather decided to take a break before continuing up the narrow road to the castle.
Look, Henry! There's a light in that tower. Maybe it's a ghost.
It's probably Carrie getting your room ready.
She said that one of the towers was just the place for four lively children.
We're so high up, Violet! Open your eyes. It's really pretty. Take a look.
I...I don't think so. Tell me when we're there.
We're there, Violet. You can look now.
Drummond Castle was not what they expected. Overgrown vines seemed to strangle the castle. Many of the stained glass windows were boarded up to protect them from damage. The whole place was gloomy.
Let's find Carrie. It will look much prettier when the fog lifts.
I guess so...I just wish it looked more like it belonged in a fairy tale instead of a--
Scary story!

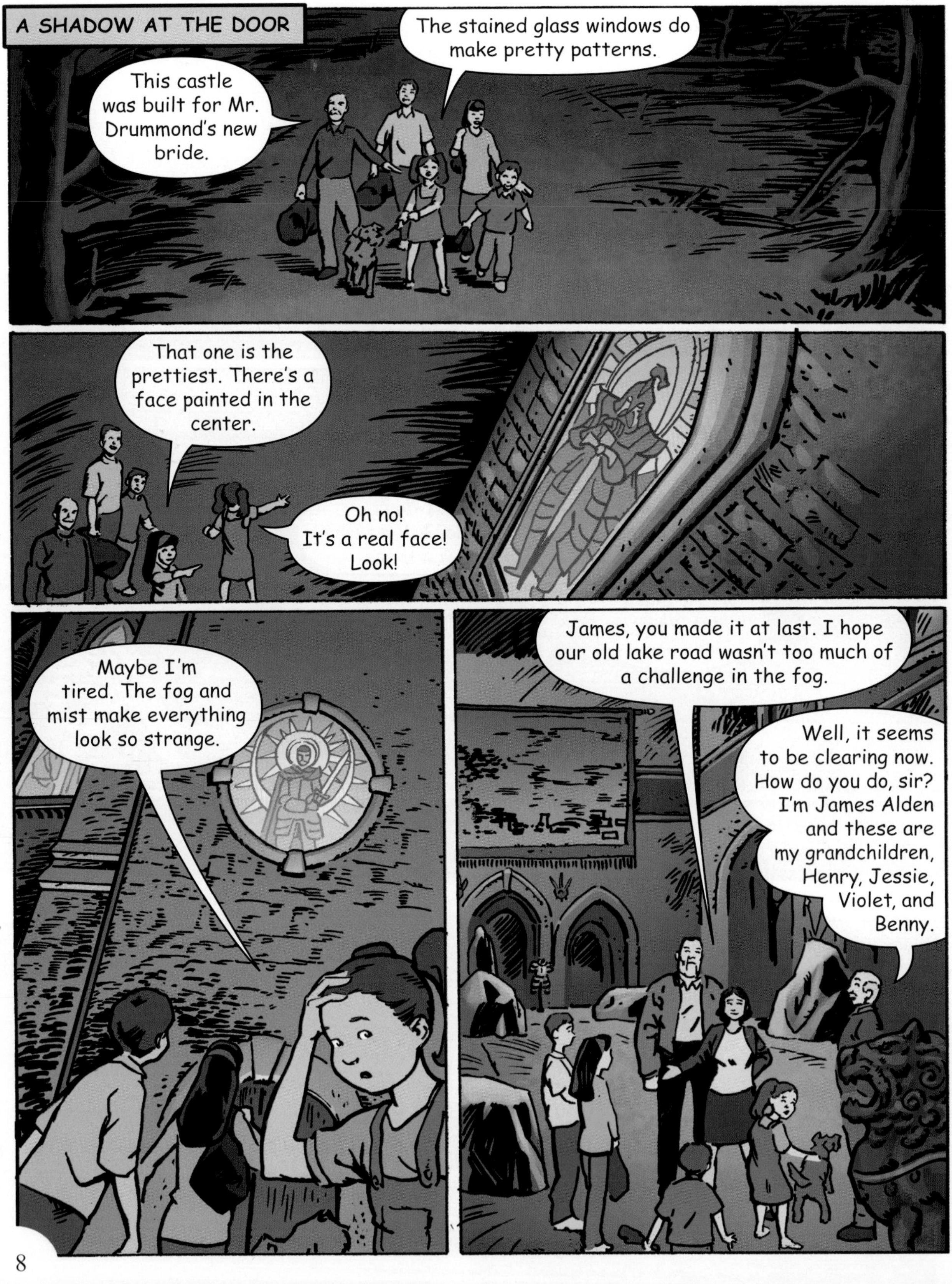
A SHADOW AT THE DOOR
This castle was built for Mr. Drummond's new bride.
The stained glass windows do make pretty patterns.
That one is the prettiest. There's a face painted in the center.
Oh no! It's a real face! Look!
Maybe I'm tired. The fog and mist make everything look so strange.
James, you made it at last. I hope our old lake road wasn't too much of a challenge in the fog.
Well, it seems to be clearing now. How do you do, sir? I'm James Alden and these are my grandchildren, Henry, Jessie, Violet, and Benny.

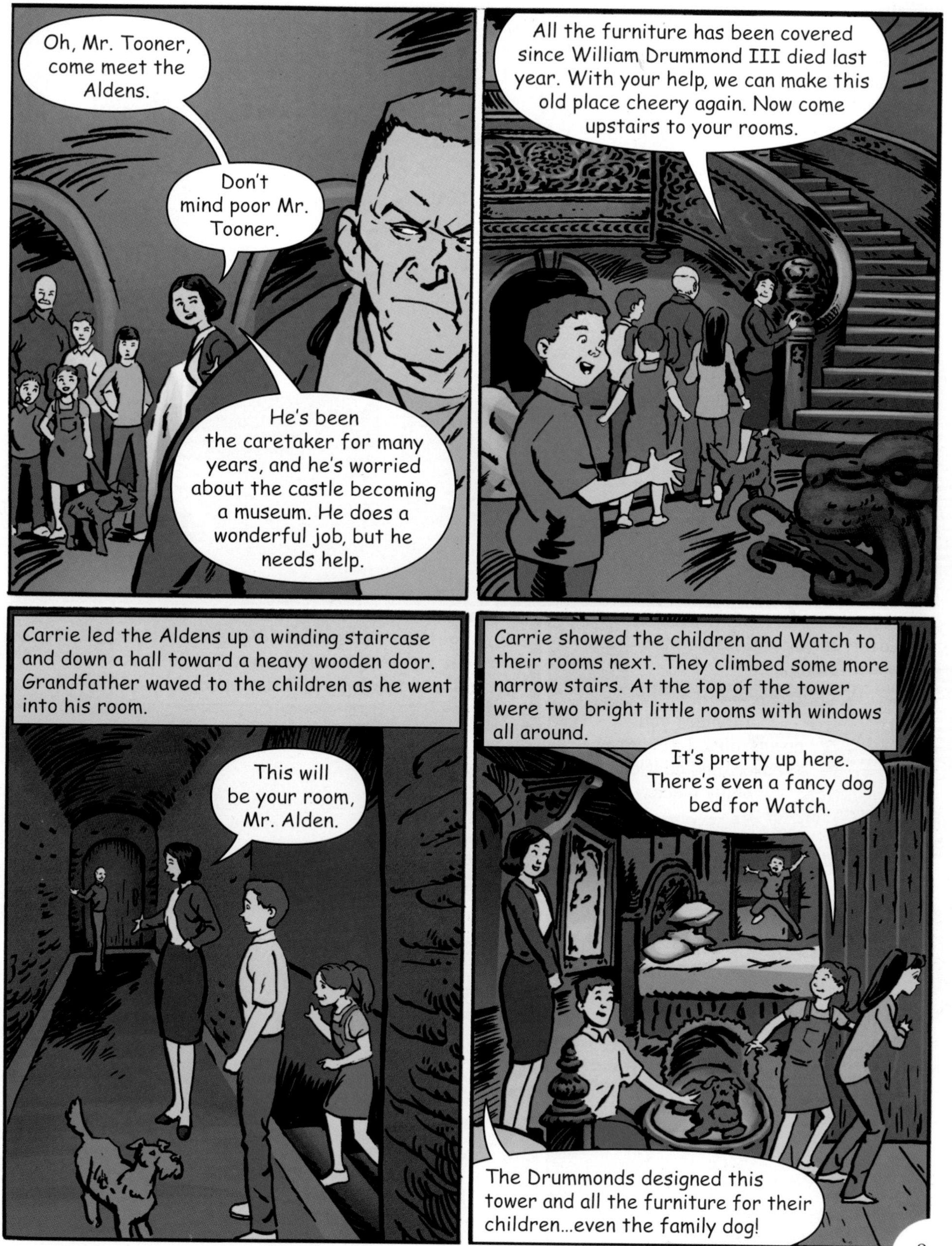

Oh, Mr. Tooner, come meet the Aldens.
Don't mind poor Mr. Tooner.
He's been the caretaker for many years, and he's worried about the castle becoming a museum. He does a wonderful job, but he needs help.
All the furniture has been covered since William Drummond III died last year. With your help, we can make this old place cheery again. Now come upstairs to your rooms.
Carrie led the Aldens up a winding staircase and down a hall toward a heavy wooden door. Grandfather waved to the children as he went into his room.
This will be your room, Mr. Alden.
Carrie showed the children and Watch to their rooms next. They climbed some more narrow stairs. At the top of the tower were two bright little rooms with windows all around.
It's pretty up here. There's even a fancy dog bed for Watch.
The Drummonds designed this tower and all the furniture for their children...even the family dog!

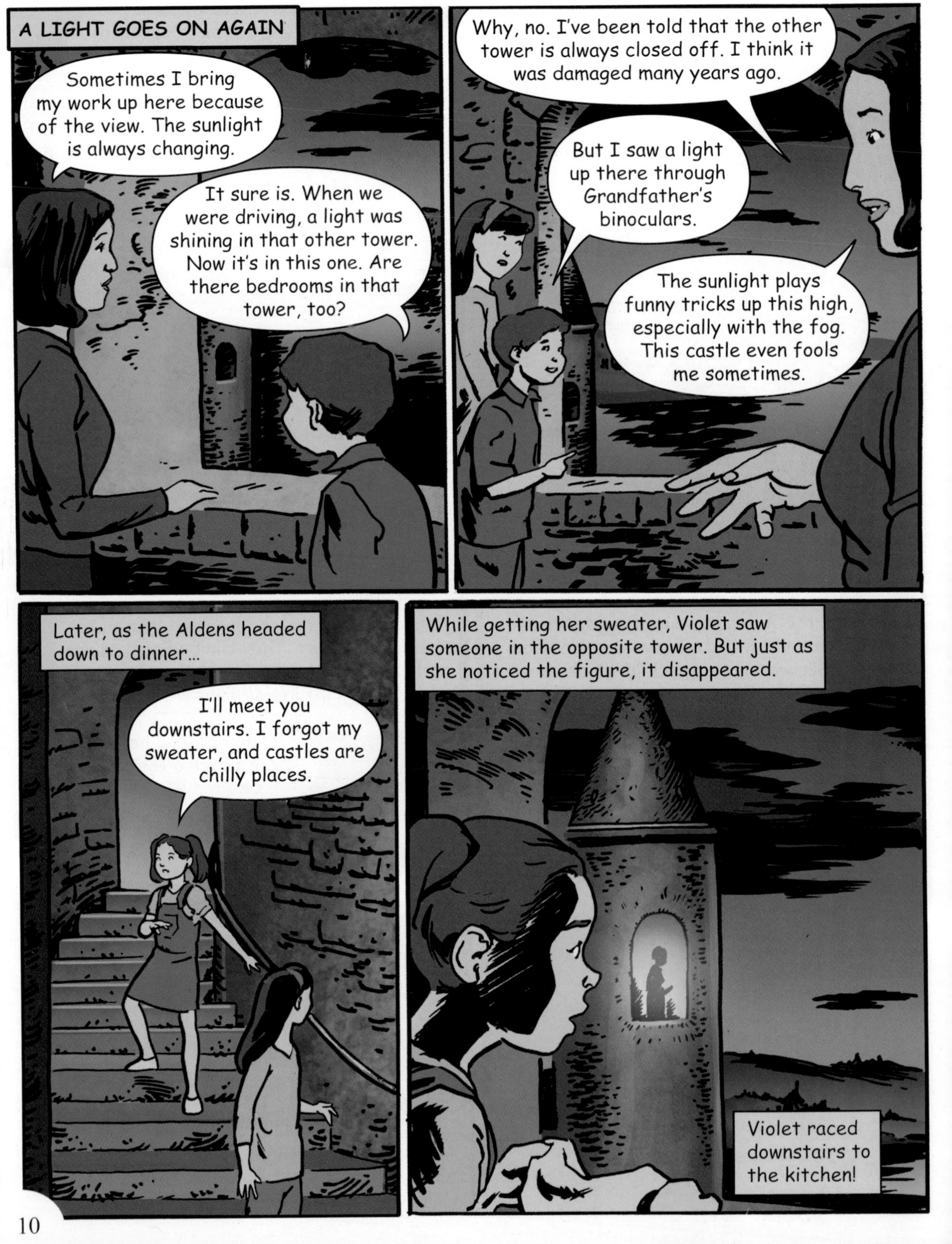
A LIGHT GOES ON AGAIN
Sometimes I bring my work up here because of the view. The sunlight is always changing.
It sure is. When we were driving, a light was shining in that other tower. Now it's in this one. Are there bedrooms in that tower, too?
Why, no. I've been told that the other tower is always closed off. I think it was damaged many years ago.
But I saw a light up there through Grandfather's binoculars.
The sunlight plays funny tricks up this high, especially with the fog. This castle even fools me sometimes.
Later, as the Aldens headed down to dinner...
I'll meet you downstairs. I forgot my sweater, and castles are chilly places.
While getting her sweater, Violet saw someone in the opposite tower. But just as she noticed the figure, it disappeared.
Violet raced downstairs to the kitchen!

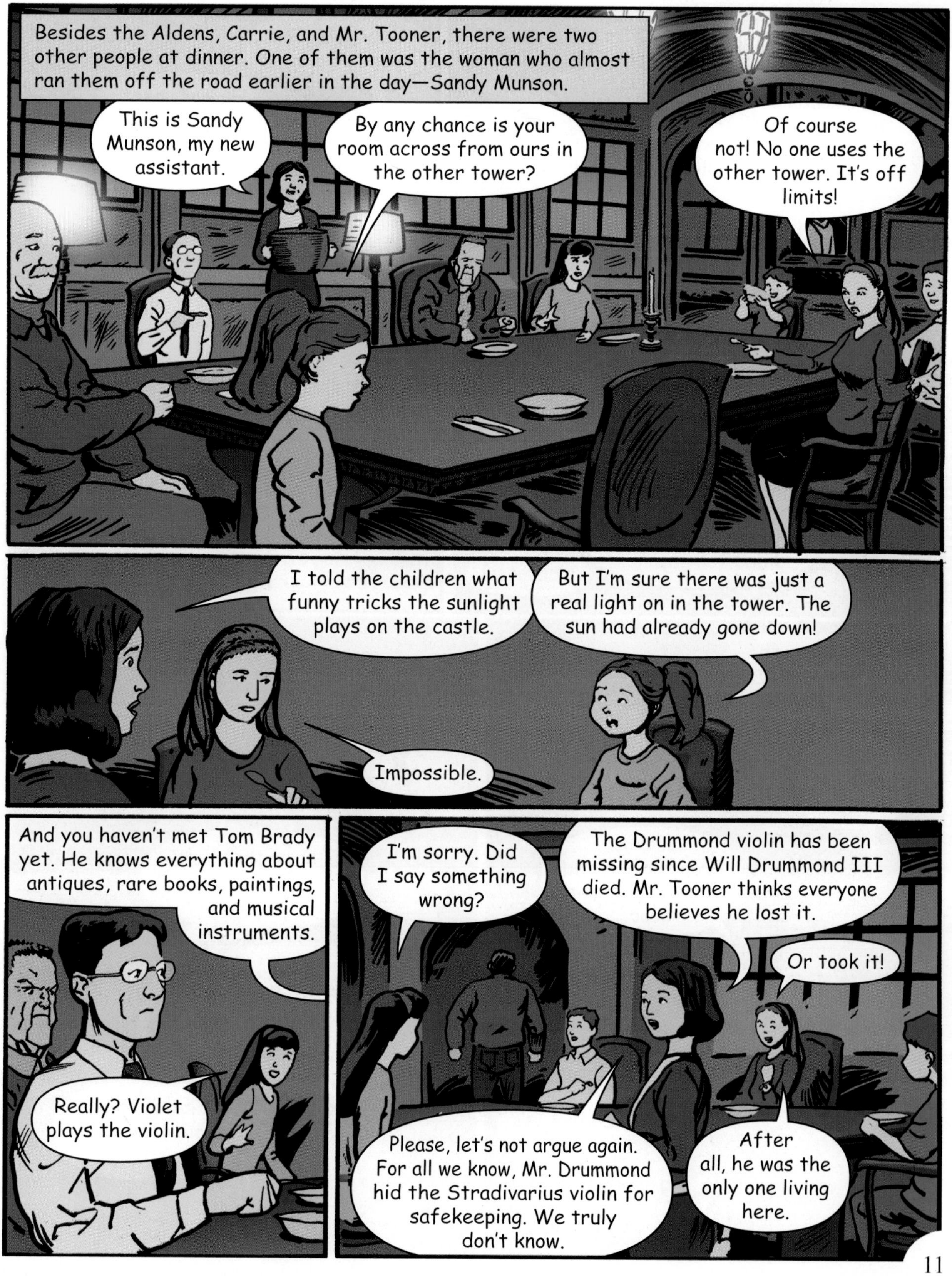

Besides the Aldens, Carrie, and Mr. Tooner, there were two other people at dinner. One of them was the woman who almost ran them off the road earlier in the day—Sandy Munson.
This is Sandy Munson, my new assistant.
By any chance is your room across from ours in the other tower?
Of course not! No one uses the other tower. It's off limits!
I told the children what funny tricks the sunlight plays on the castle.
But I'm sure there was just a real light on in the tower. The sun had already gone down!
Impossible.
And you haven't met Tom Brady yet. He knows everything about antiques, rare books, paintings, and musical instruments.
Really? Violet plays the violin.
I'm sorry. Did I say something wrong?
The Drummond violin has been missing since Will Drummond III died. Mr. Tooner thinks everyone believes he lost it.
Or took it!
Please, let's not argue again. For all we know, Mr. Drummond hid the Stradivarius violin for safekeeping. We truly don't know.
After all, he was the only one living here.

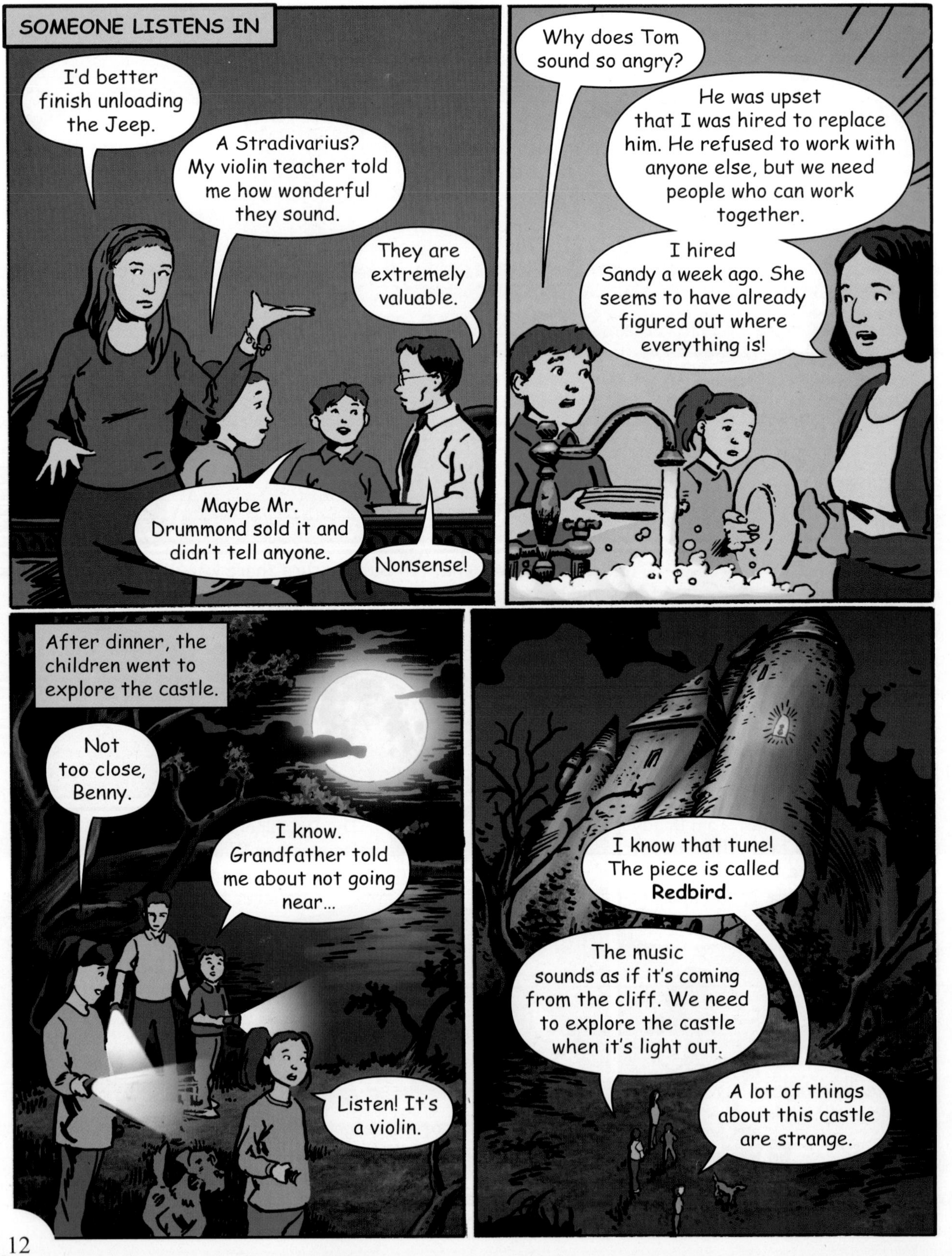
SOMEONE LISTENS IN
I'd better finish unloading the Jeep.
A Stradivarius? My violin teacher told me how wonderful they sound.
They are extremely valuable.
Maybe Mr. Drummond sold it and didn't tell anyone.
Nonsense!
Why does Tom sound so angry?
He was upset that I was hired to replace him. He refused to work with anyone else, but we need people who can work together.
I hired Sandy a week ago. She seems to have already figured out where everything is!
After dinner, the children went to explore the castle.
Not too close, Benny.
I know. Grandfather told me about not going near...
Listen! It's a violin.
I know that tune! The piece is called **Redbird.**
The music sounds as if it's coming from the cliff. We need to explore the castle when it's light out.
A lot of things about this castle are strange.

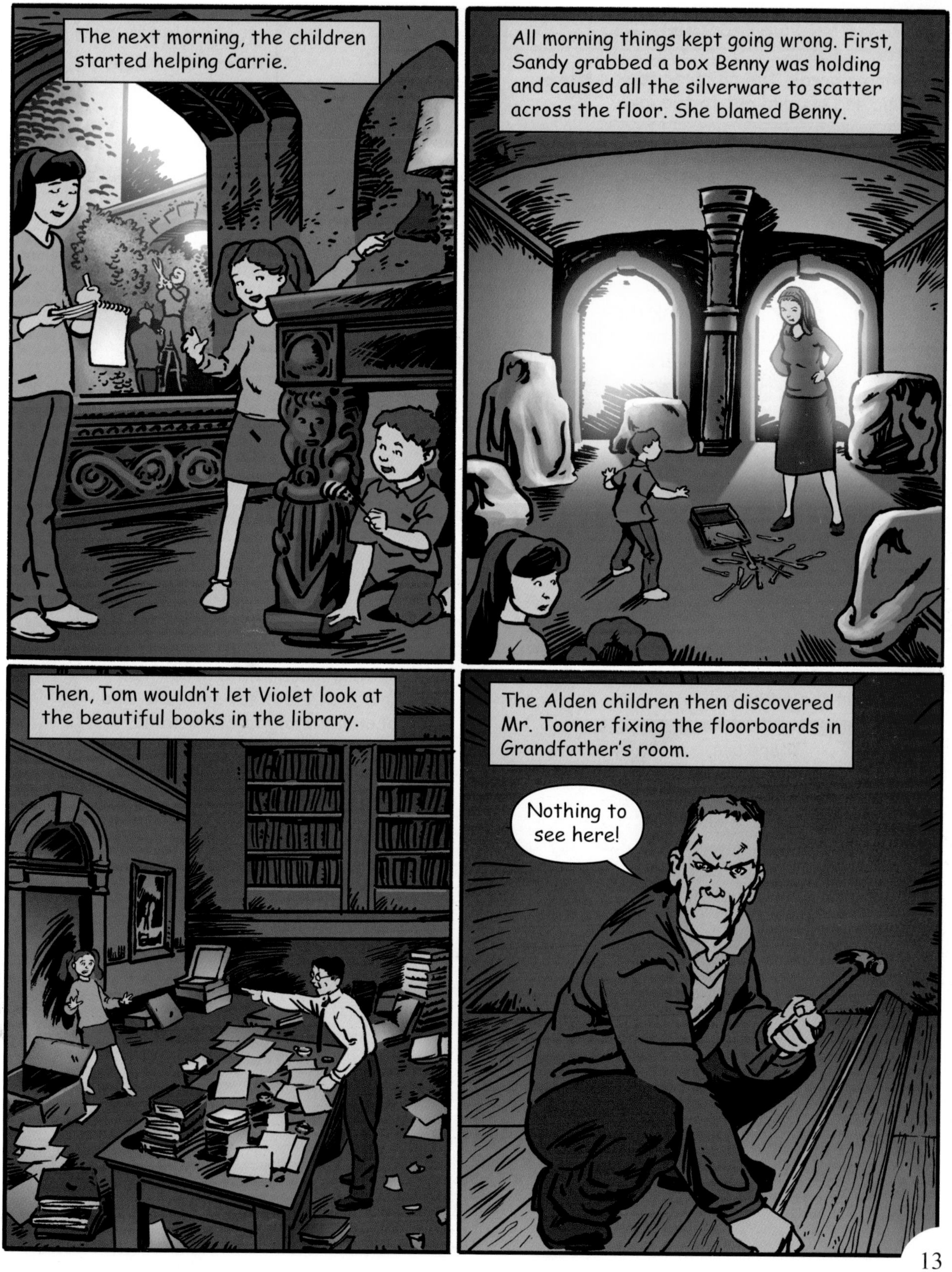
The next morning, the children started helping Carrie.
All morning things kept going wrong. First, Sandy grabbed a box Benny was holding and caused all the silverware to scatter across the floor. She blamed Benny.
Then, Tom wouldn't let Violet look at the beautiful books in the library.
The Alden children then discovered Mr. Tooner fixing the floorboards in Grandfather's room.
Nothing to see here!

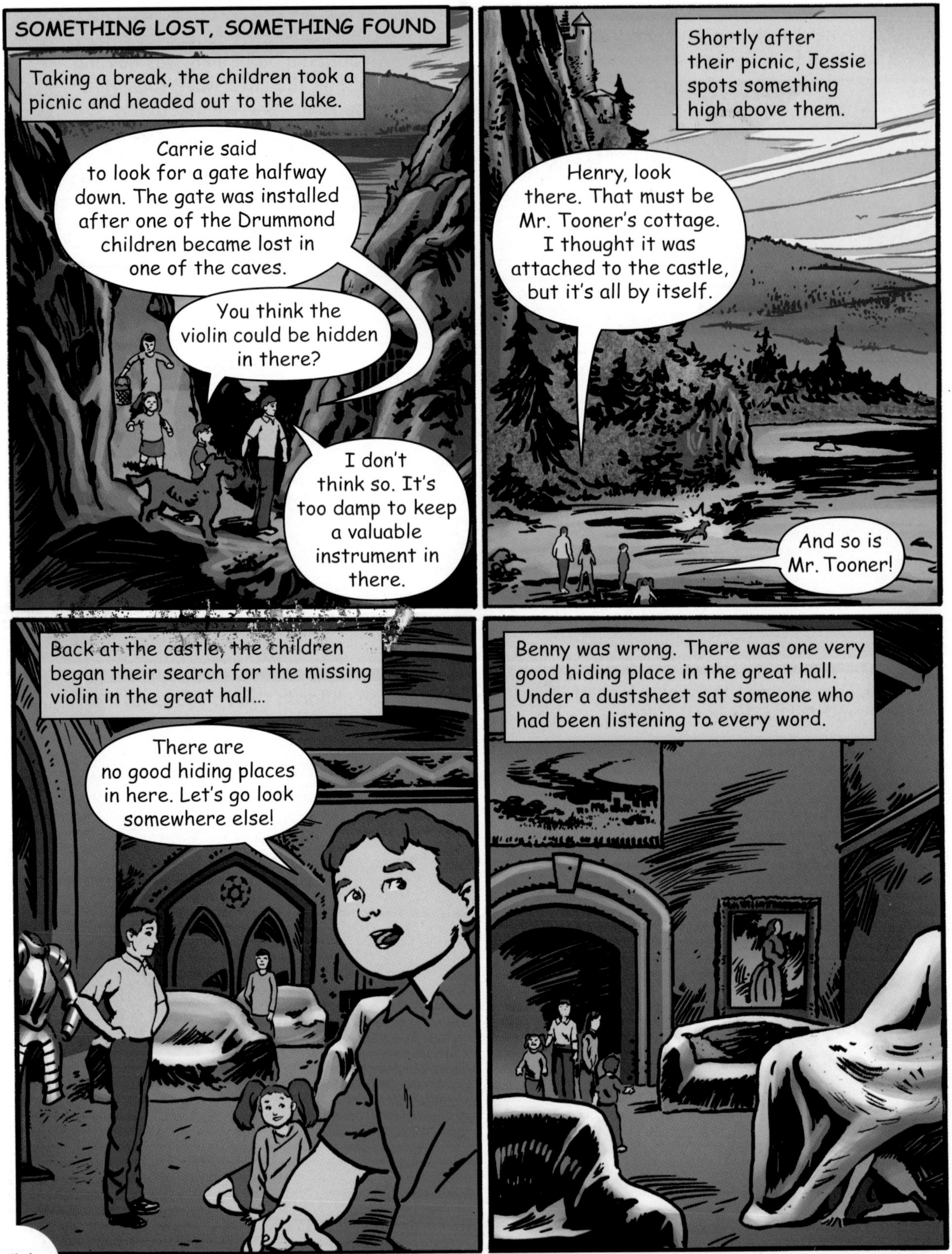
SOMETHING LOST, SOMETHING FOUND
Taking a break, the children took a picnic and headed out to the lake.
Carrie said to look for a gate halfway down. The gate was installed after one of the Drummond children became lost in one of the caves.
You think the violin could be hidden in there?
I don't think so. It's too damp to keep a valuable instrument in there.
Shortly after their picnic, Jessie spots something high above them.
Henry, look there. That must be Mr. Tooner's cottage. I thought it was attached to the castle, but it's all by itself.
And so is Mr. Tooner!
Back at the castle, the children began their search for the missing violin in the great hall...
There are no good hiding places in here. Let's go look somewhere else!
Benny was wrong. There was one very good hiding place in the great hall. Under a dustsheet sat someone who had been listening to every word.

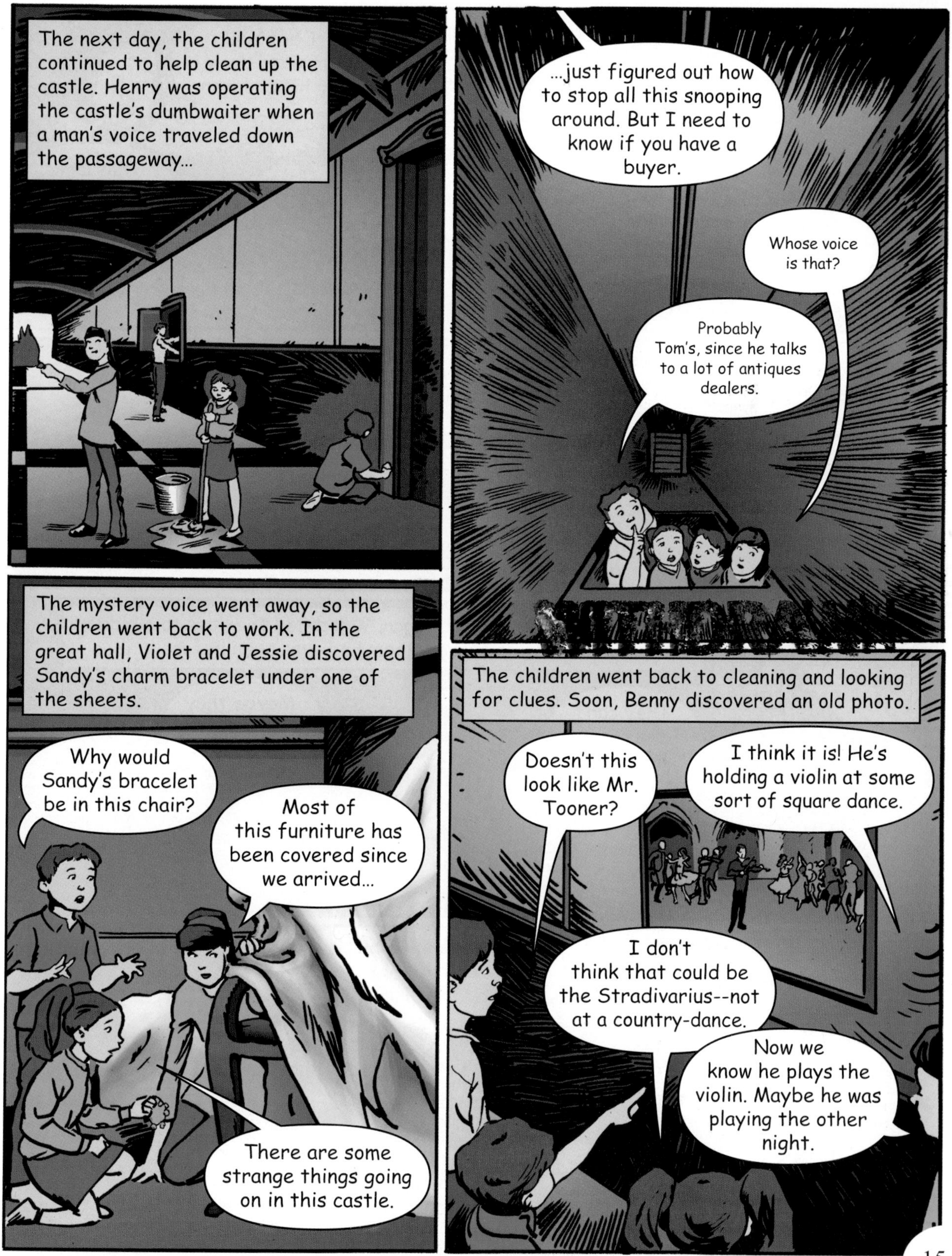
The next day, the children continued to help clean up the castle. Henry was operating the castle's dumbwaiter when a man's voice traveled down the passageway...
...just figured out how to stop all this snooping around. But I need to know if you have a buyer.
Whose voice is that?
Probably Tom's, since he talks to a lot of antiques dealers.
The mystery voice went away, so the children went back to work. In the great hall, Violet and Jessie discovered Sandy's charm bracelet under one of the sheets.
Why would Sandy's bracelet be in this chair?
Most of this furniture has been covered since we arrived...
There are some strange things going on in this castle.
The children went back to cleaning and looking for clues. Soon, Benny discovered an old photo.
Doesn't this look like Mr. Tooner?
I think it is! He's holding a violin at some sort of square dance.
I don't think that could be the Stradivarius--not at a country-dance.
Now we know he plays the violin. Maybe he was playing the other night.

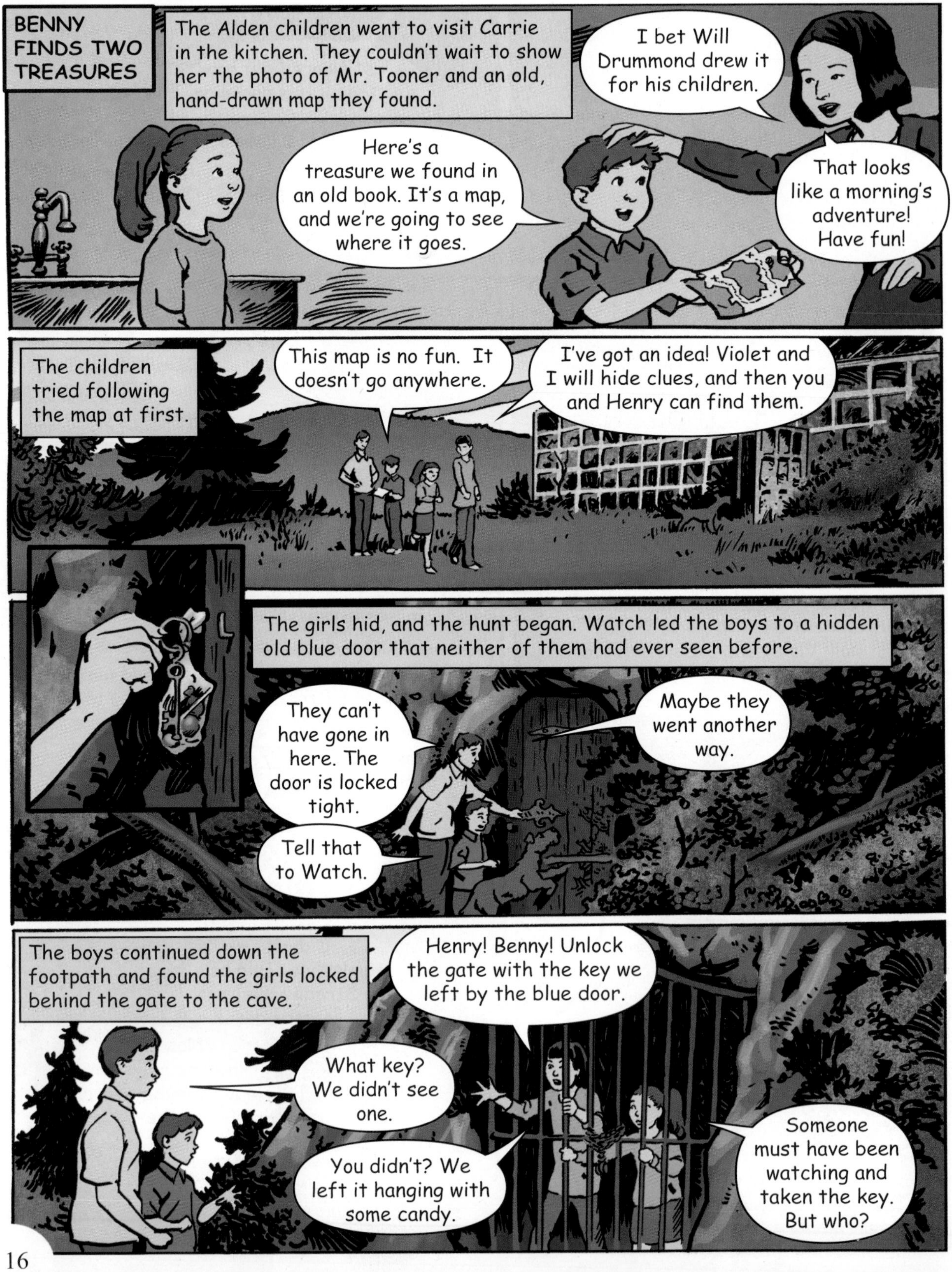
BENNY FINDS TWO TREASURES
The Alden children went to visit Carrie in the kitchen. They couldn't wait to show her the photo of Mr. Tooner and an old, hand-drawn map they found.
I bet Will Drummond drew it for his children.
Here's a treasure we found in an old book. It's a map, and we're going to see where it goes.
That looks like a morning's adventure! Have fun!
The children tried following the map at first.
This map is no fun. It doesn't go anywhere.
I've got an idea! Violet and I will hide clues, and then you and Henry can find them.
The girls hid, and the hunt began. Watch led the boys to a hidden old blue door that neither of them had ever seen before.
They can't have gone in here. The door is locked tight.
Maybe they went another way.
Tell that to Watch.
The boys continued down the footpath and found the girls locked behind the gate to the cave.
Henry! Benny! Unlock the gate with the key we left by the blue door.
What key? We didn't see one.
You didn't? We left it hanging with some candy.
Someone must have been watching and taken the key. But who?

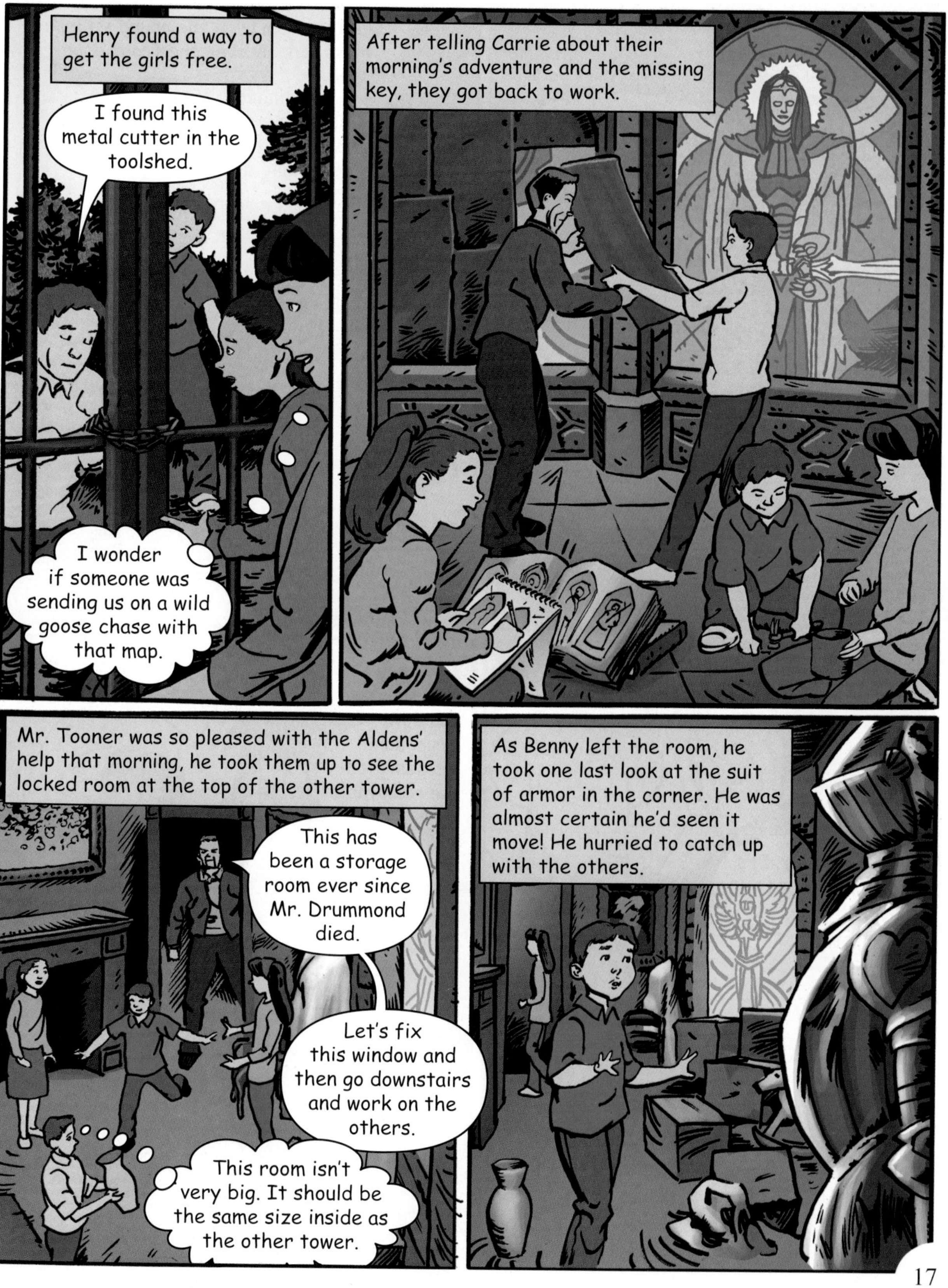
Henry found a way to get the girls free.
I found this metal cutter in the toolshed.
I wonder if someone was sending us on a wild goose chase with that map.
After telling Carrie about their morning's adventure and the missing key, they got back to work.
Mr. Tooner was so pleased with the Aldens' help that morning, he took them up to see the locked room at the top of the other tower.
This has been a storage room ever since Mr. Drummond died.
Let's fix this window and then go downstairs and work on the others.
This room isn't very big. It should be the same size inside as the other tower.
As Benny left the room, he took one last look at the suit of armor in the corner. He was almost certain he'd seen it move! He hurried to catch up with the others.

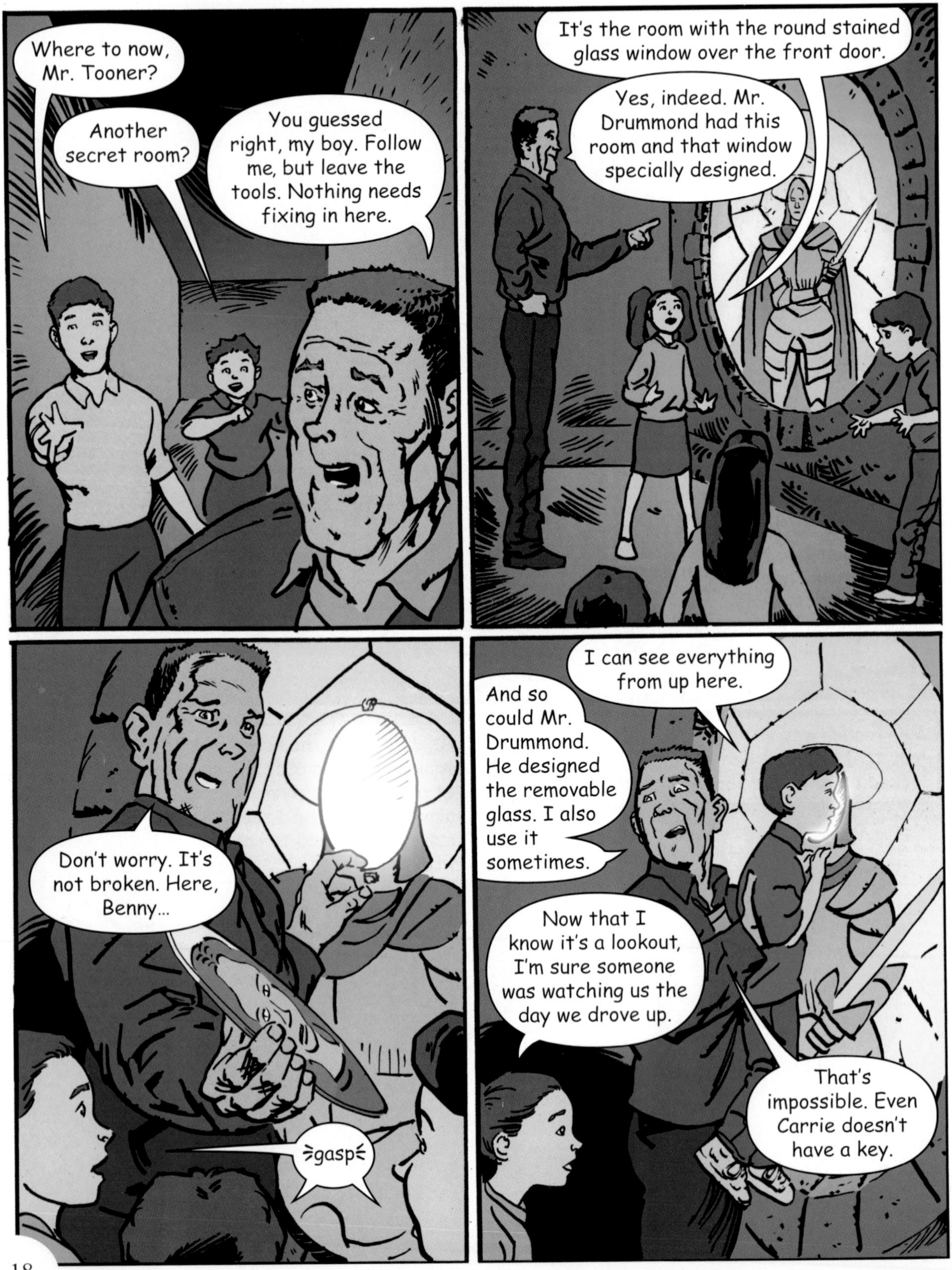
Where to now, Mr. Tooner?
Another secret room?
You guessed right, my boy. Follow me, but leave the tools. Nothing needs fixing in here.
It's the room with the round stained glass window over the front door.
Yes, indeed. Mr. Drummond had this room and that window specially designed.
Don't worry. It's not broken. Here, Benny...
gasp
I can see everything from up here.
And so could Mr. Drummond. He designed the removable glass. I also use it sometimes.
Now that I know it's a lookout, I'm sure someone was watching us the day we drove up.
That's impossible. Even Carrie doesn't have a key.

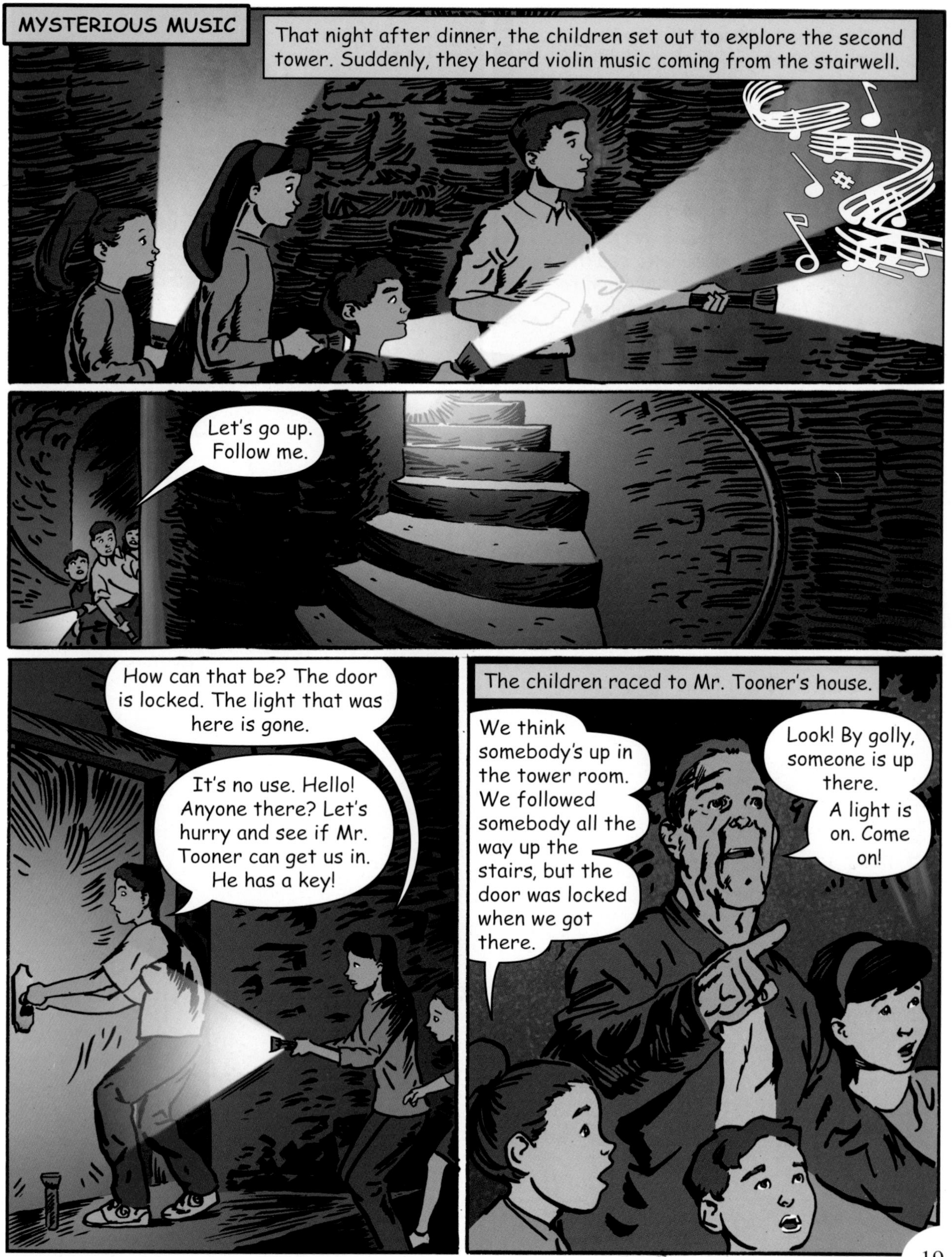
MYSTERIOUS MUSIC
That night after dinner, the children set out to explore the second tower. Suddenly, they heard violin music coming from the stairwell.
Let's go up. Follow me.
How can that be? The door is locked. The light that was here is gone.
It's no use. Hello! Anyone there? Let's hurry and see if Mr. Tooner can get us in. He has a key!
The children raced to Mr. Tooner's house.
We think somebody's up in the tower room. We followed somebody all the way up the stairs, but the door was locked when we got there.
Look! By golly, someone is up there.
A light is on. Come on!

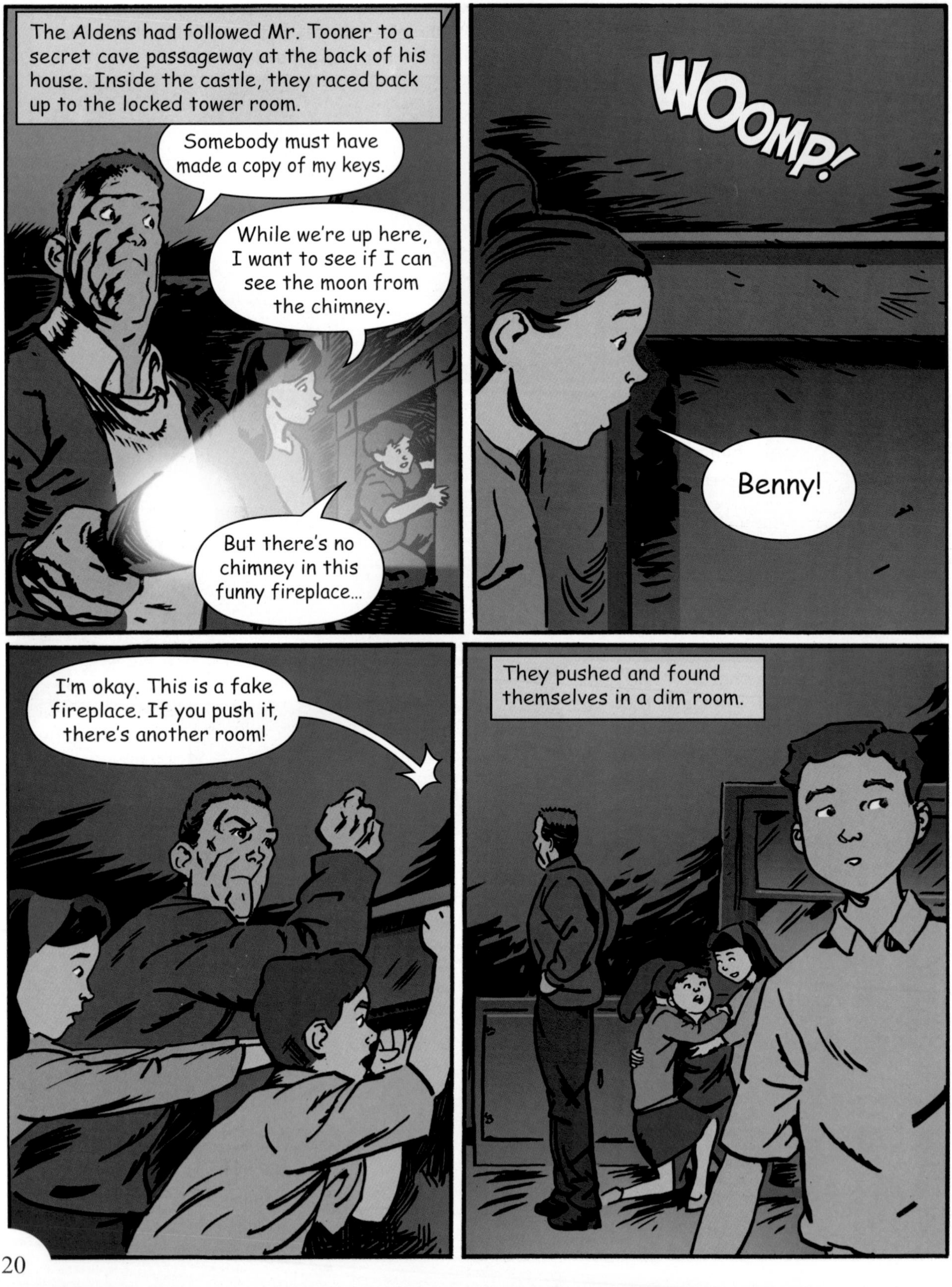

The Aldens had followed Mr. Tooner to a secret cave passageway at the back of his house. Inside the castle, they raced back up to the locked tower room.
Somebody must have made a copy of my keys.
While we're up here, I want to see if I can see the moon from the chimney.
But there's no chimney in this funny fireplace...
WOOMP!
Benny!
I'm okay. This is a fake fireplace. If you push it, there's another room!
They pushed and found themselves in a dim room.

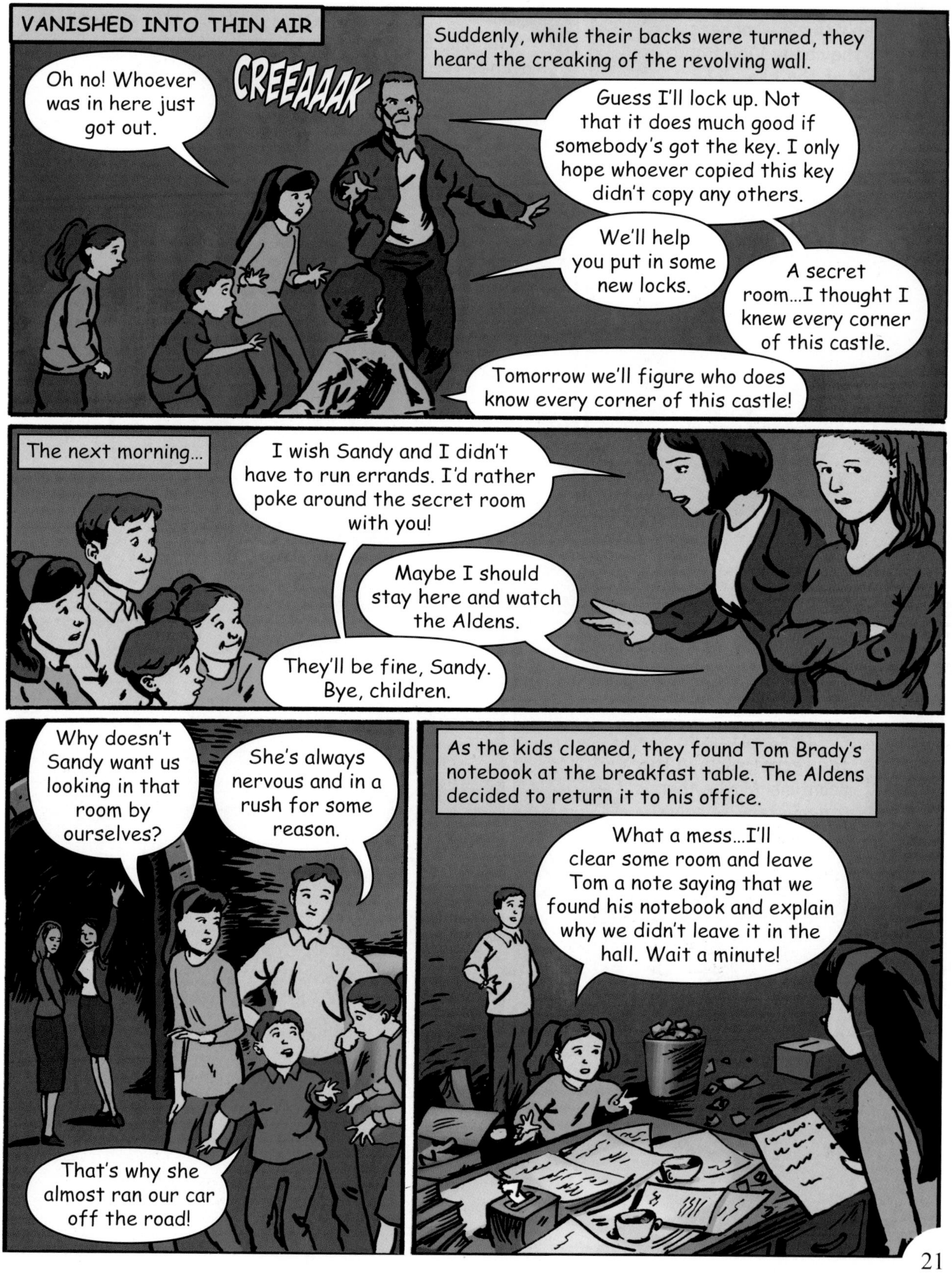
VANISHED INTO THIN AIR
Suddenly, while their backs were turned, they heard the creaking of the revolving wall.
CREEAAAK
Oh no! Whoever was in here just got out.
Guess I'll lock up. Not that it does much good if somebody's got the key. I only hope whoever copied this key didn't copy any others.
We'll help you put in some new locks.
A secret room...I thought I knew every corner of this castle.
Tomorrow we'll figure who does know every corner of this castle!
The next morning...
I wish Sandy and I didn't have to run errands. I'd rather poke around the secret room with you!
Maybe I should stay here and watch the Aldens.
They'll be fine, Sandy. Bye, children.
Why doesn't Sandy want us looking in that room by ourselves?
She's always nervous and in a rush for some reason.
That's why she almost ran our car off the road!
As the kids cleaned, they found Tom Brady's notebook at the breakfast table. The Aldens decided to return it to his office.
What a mess...I'll clear some room and leave Tom a note saying that we found his notebook and explain why we didn't leave it in the hall. Wait a minute!

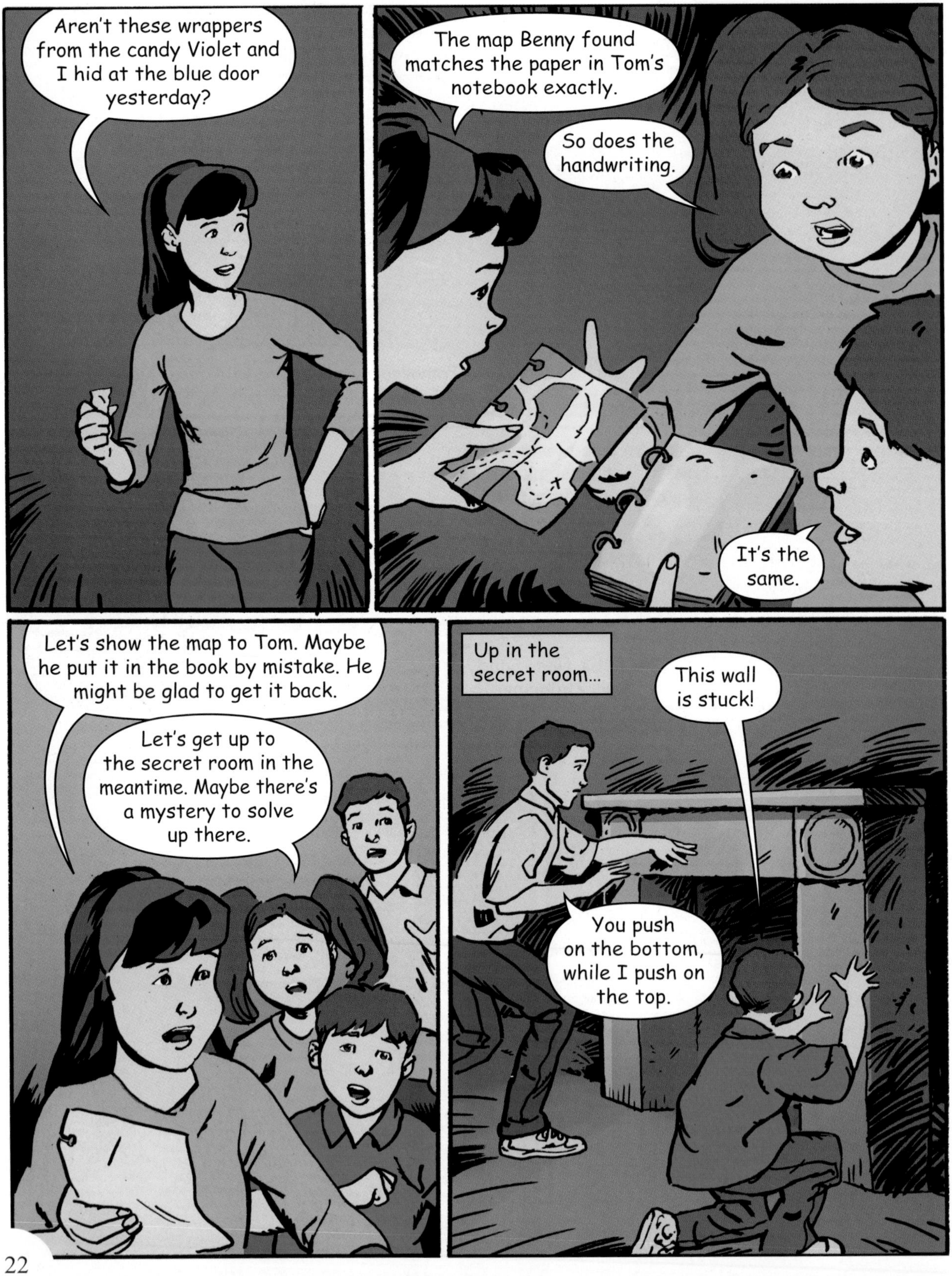
Aren't these wrappers from the candy Violet and I hid at the blue door yesterday?
The map Benny found matches the paper in Tom's notebook exactly.
So does the handwriting.
It's the same.
Let's show the map to Tom. Maybe he put it in the book by mistake. He might be glad to get it back.
Let's get up to the secret room in the meantime. Maybe there's a mystery to solve up there.
Up in the secret room...
This wall is stuck!
You push on the bottom, while I push on the top.

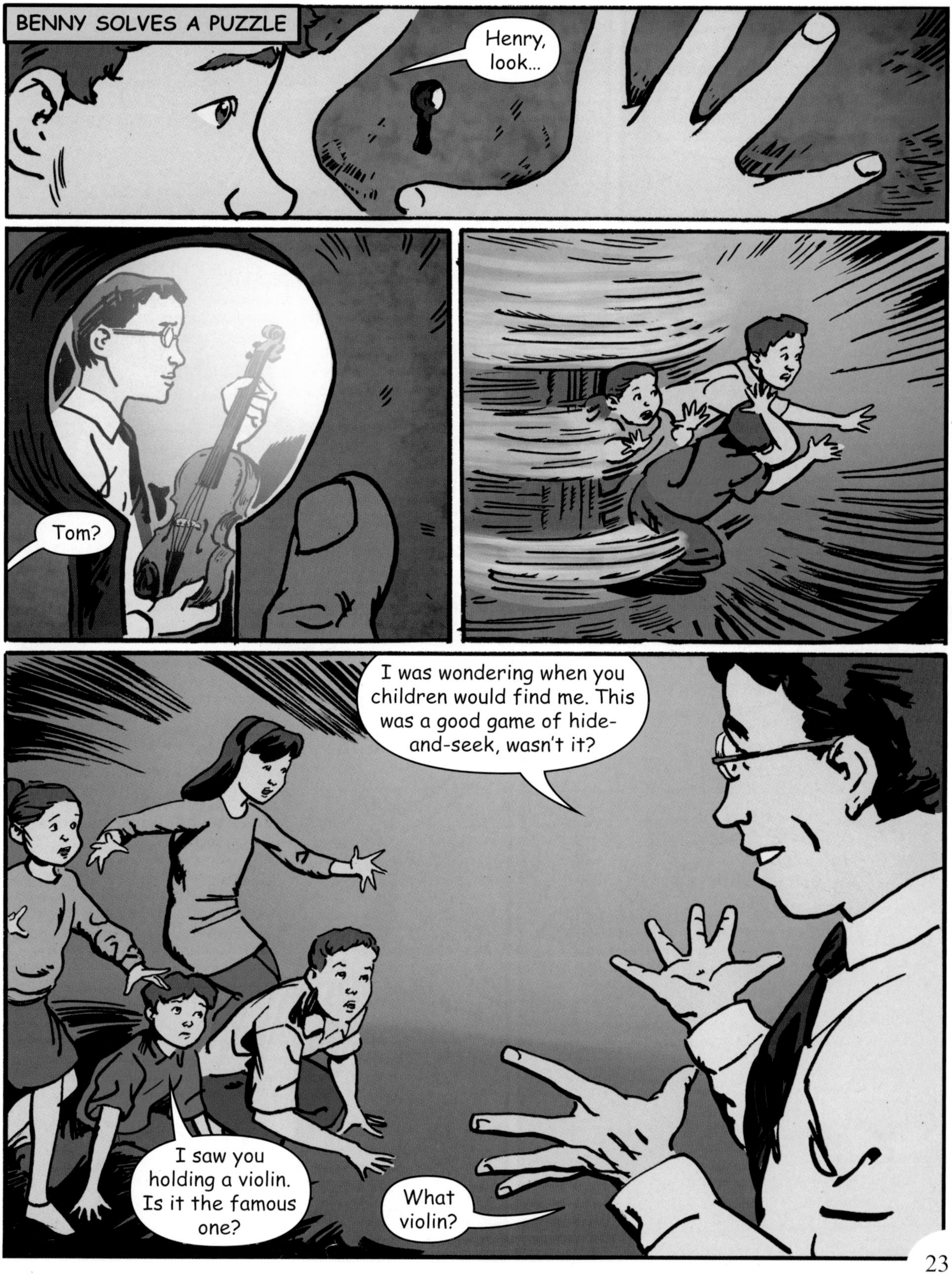
BENNY SOLVES A PUZZLE
Henry, look...
Tom?
I was wondering when you children would find me. This was a good game of hide-and-seek, wasn't it?
I saw you holding a violin. Is it the famous one?
What violin?

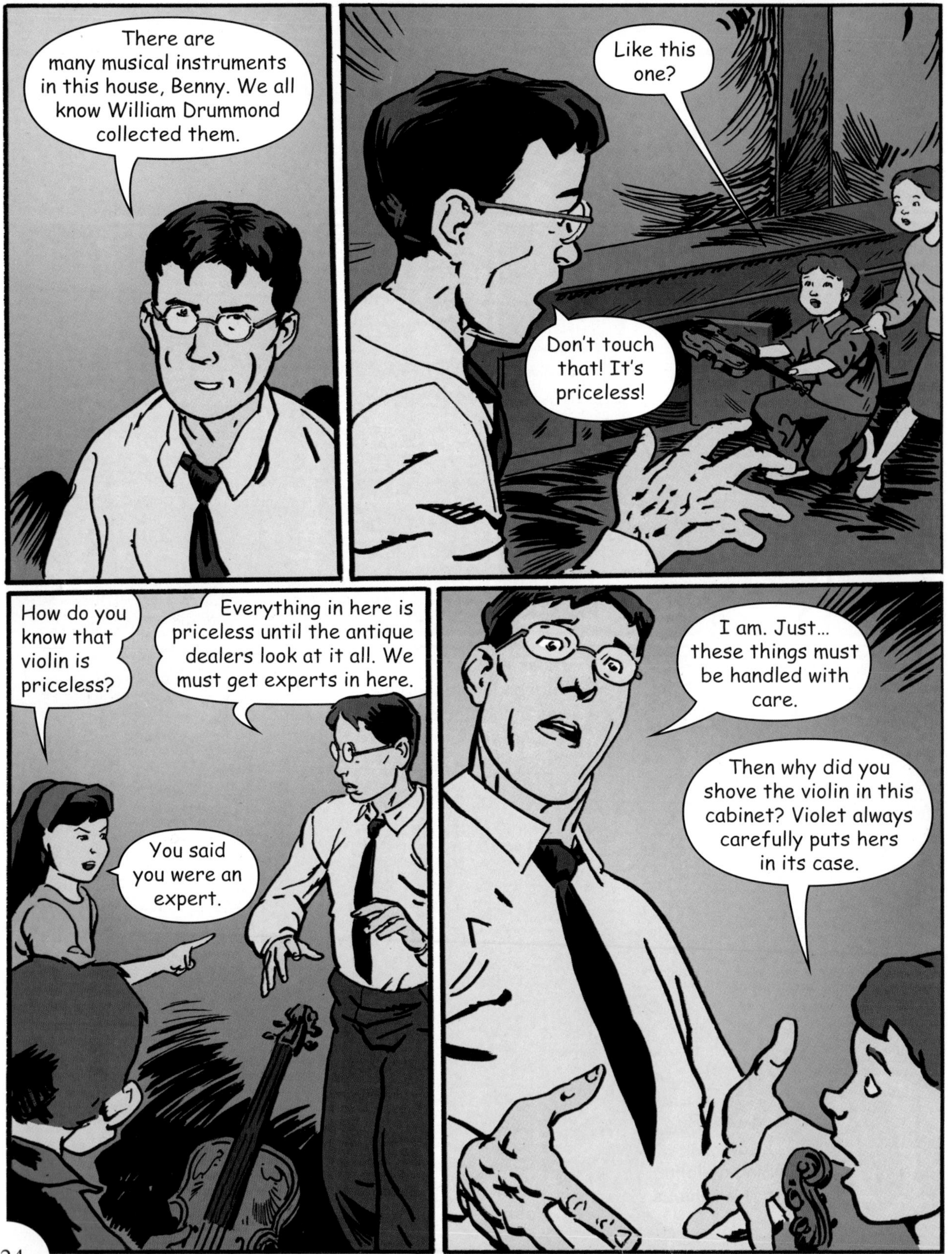
There are many musical instruments in this house, Benny. We all know William Drummond collected them.
Like this one?
Don't touch that! It's priceless!
How do you know that violin is priceless?
Everything in here is priceless until the antique dealers look at it all. We must get experts in here.
You said you were an expert.
I am. Just... these things must be handled with care.
Then why did you shove the violin in this cabinet? Violet always carefully puts hers in its case.

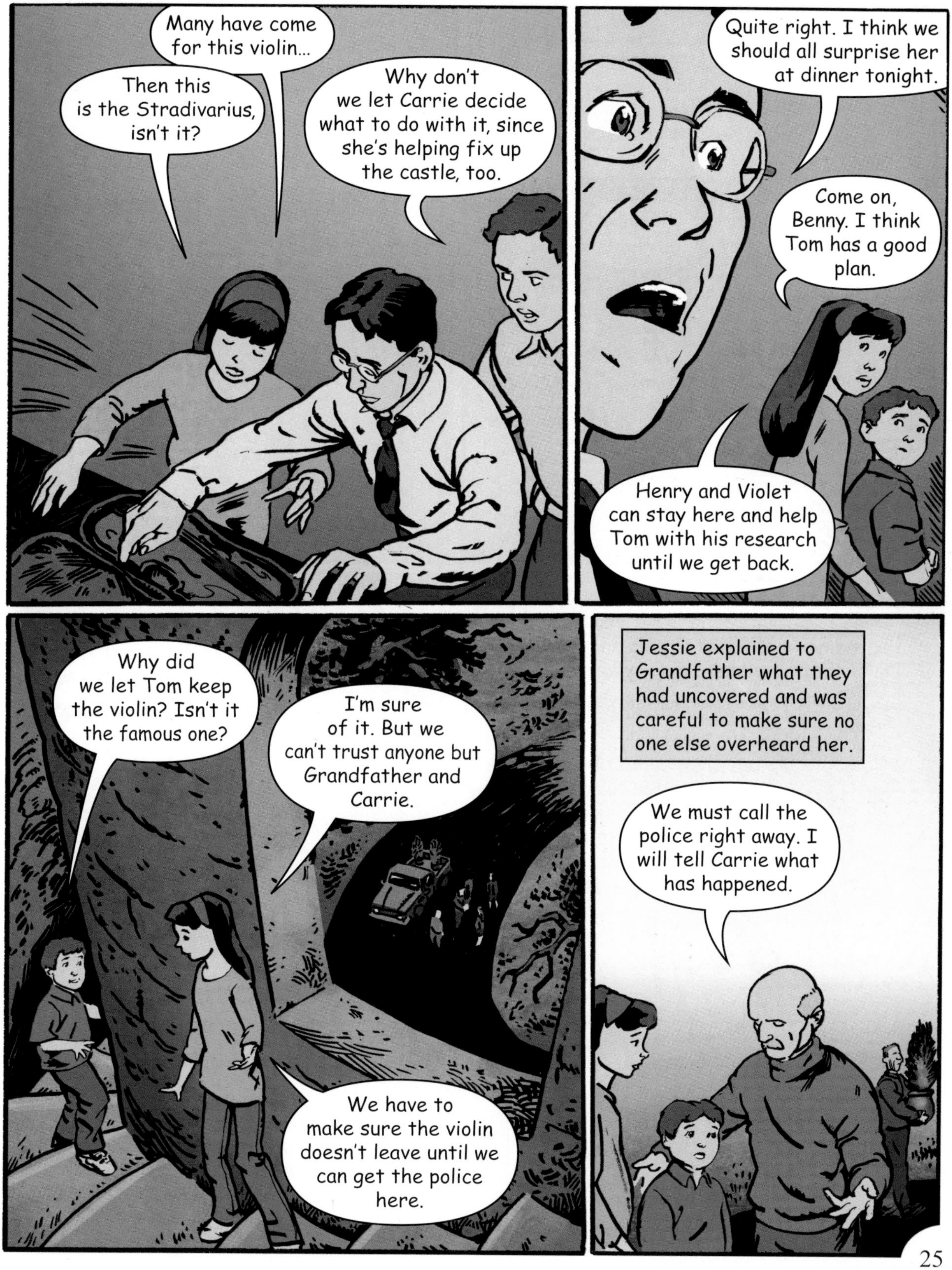
Many have come for this violin...
Then this is the Stradivarius, isn't it?
Why don't we let Carrie decide what to do with it, since she's helping fix up the castle, too.
Quite right. I think we should all surprise her at dinner tonight.
Come on, Benny. I think Tom has a good plan.
Henry and Violet can stay here and help Tom with his research until we get back.
Why did we let Tom keep the violin? Isn't it the famous one?
I'm sure of it. But we can't trust anyone but Grandfather and Carrie.
We have to make sure the violin doesn't leave until we can get the police here.
Jessie explained to Grandfather what they had uncovered and was careful to make sure no one else overheard her.
We must call the police right away. I will tell Carrie what has happened.

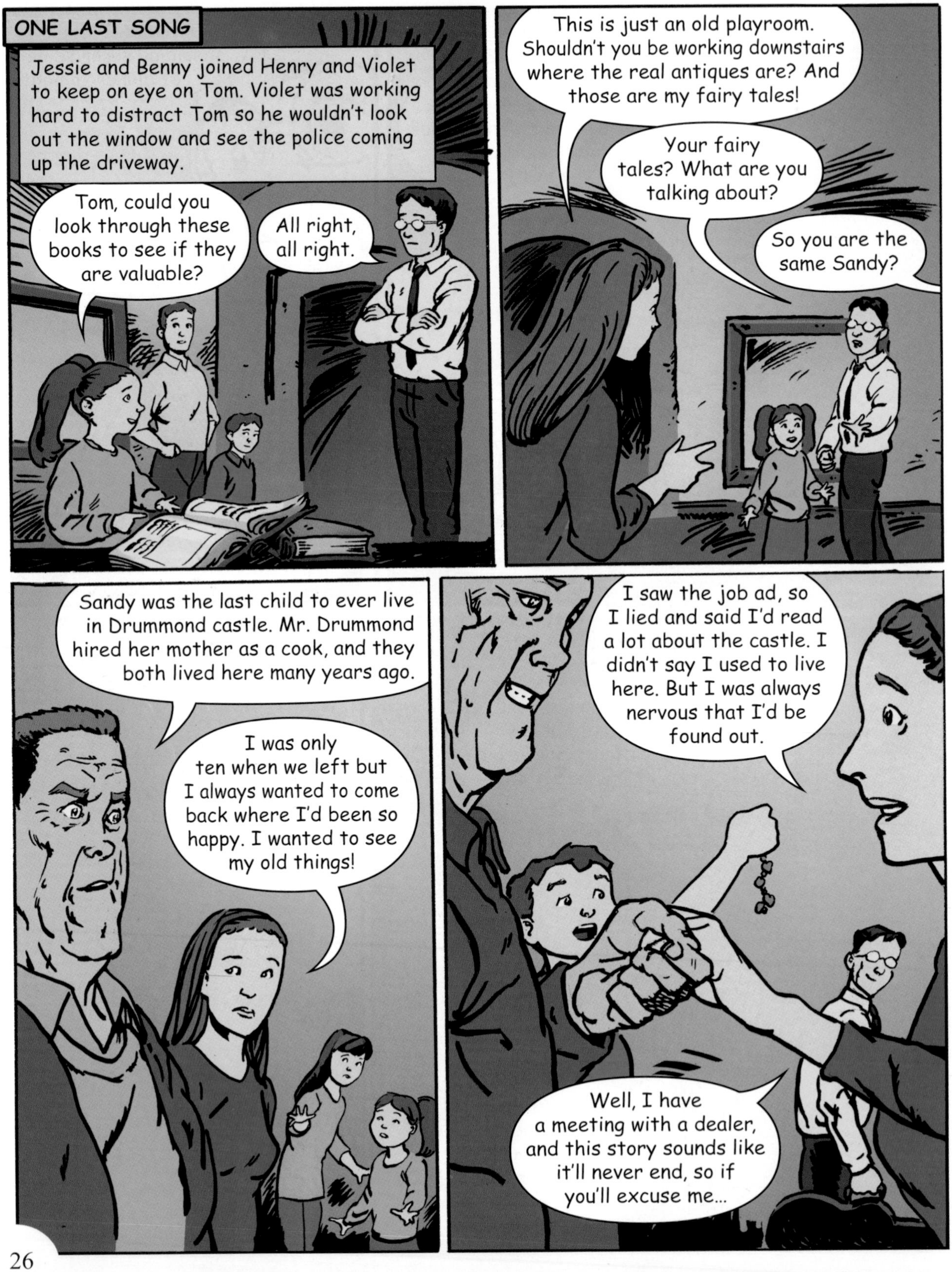
ONE LAST SONG
Jessie and Benny joined Henry and Violet to keep on eye on Tom. Violet was working hard to distract Tom so he wouldn't look out the window and see the police coming up the driveway.
Tom, could you look through these books to see if they are valuable?
All right, all right.
This is just an old playroom. Shouldn't you be working downstairs where the real antiques are? And those are my fairy tales!
Your fairy tales? What are you talking about?
So you are the same Sandy?
Sandy was the last child to ever live in Drummond castle. Mr. Drummond hired her mother as a cook, and they both lived here many years ago.
I was only ten when we left but I always wanted to come back where I'd been so happy. I wanted to see my old things!
I saw the job ad, so I lied and said I'd read a lot about the castle. I didn't say I used to live here. But I was always nervous that I'd be found out.
Well, I have a meeting with a dealer, and this story sounds like it'll never end, so if you'll excuse me...

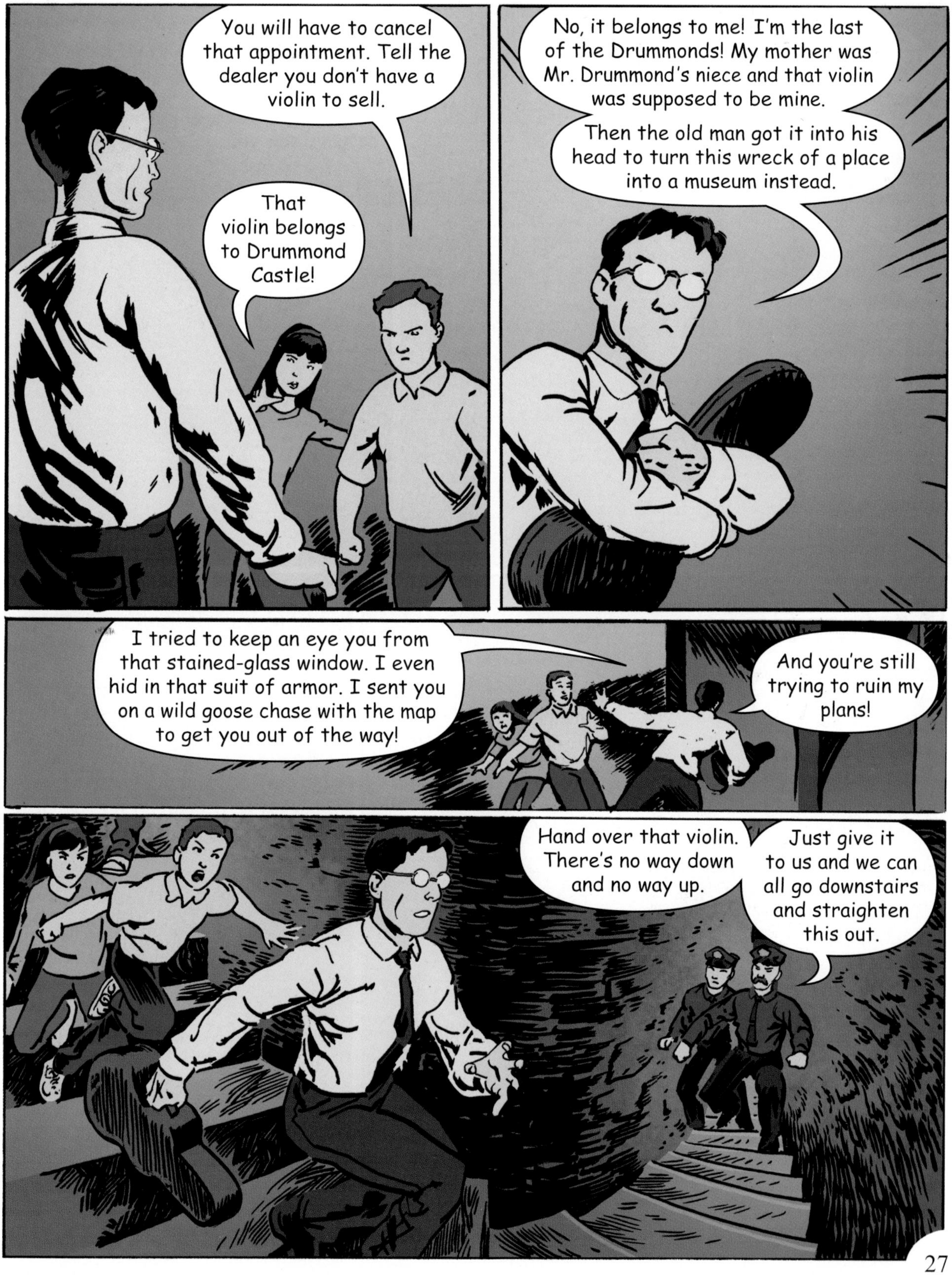

You will have to cancel that appointment. Tell the dealer you don't have a violin to sell.
That violin belongs to Drummond Castle!
No, it belongs to me! I'm the last of the Drummonds! My mother was Mr. Drummond's niece and that violin was supposed to be mine.
Then the old man got it into his head to turn this wreck of a place into a museum instead.
I tried to keep an eye you from that stained-glass window. I even hid in that suit of armor. I sent you on a wild goose chase with the map to get you out of the way!
And you're still trying to ruin my plans!
Hand over that violin. There's no way down and no way up.
Just give it to us and we can all go downstairs and straighten this out.

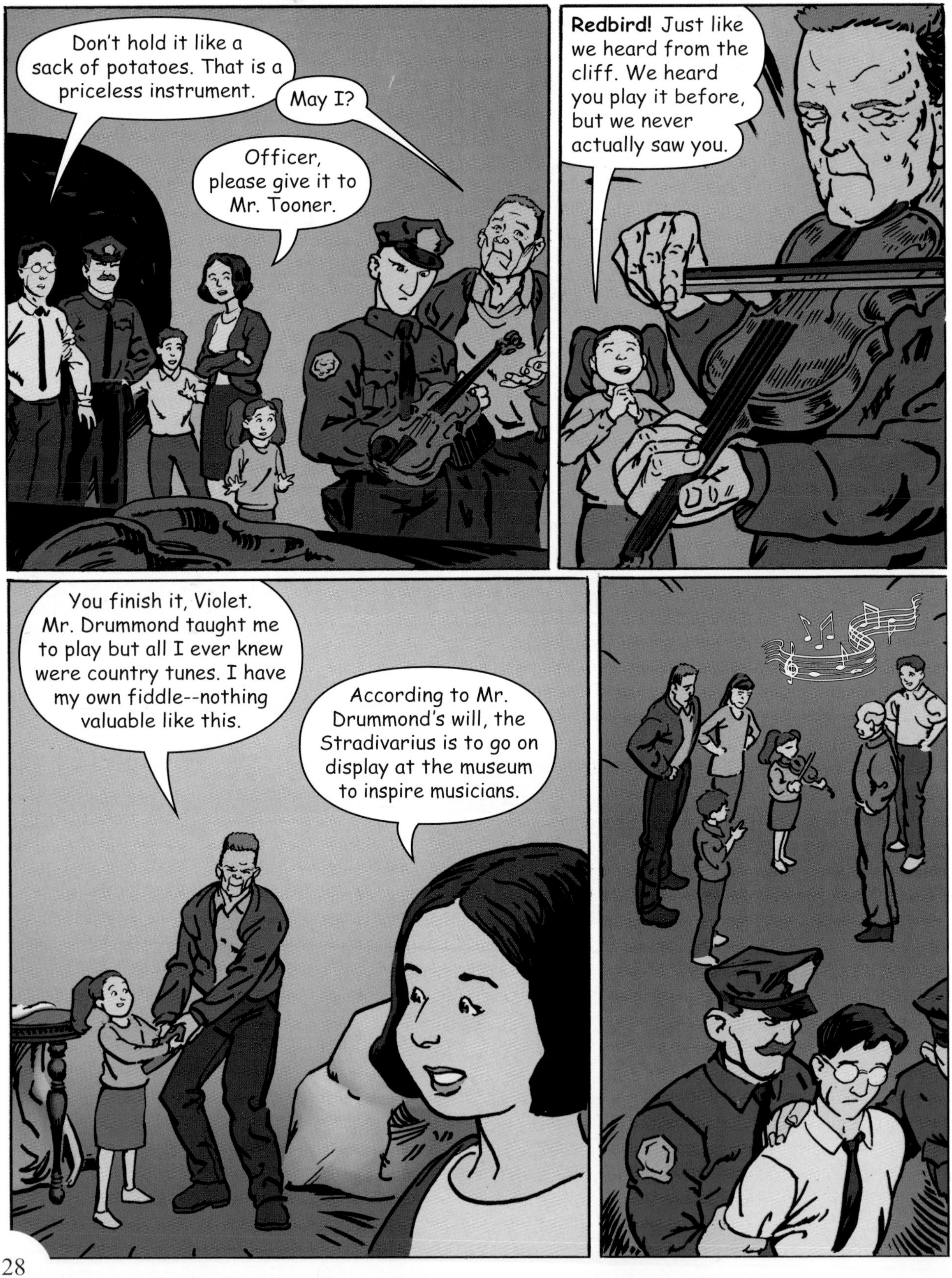

Don't hold it like a sack of potatoes. That is a priceless instrument.
May I?
Officer, please give it to Mr. Tooner.
Redbird! Just like we heard from the cliff. We heard you play it before, but we never actually saw you.
You finish it, Violet. Mr. Drummond taught me to play but all I ever knew were country tunes. I have my own fiddle--nothing valuable like this.
According to Mr. Drummond's will, the Stradivarius is to go on display at the museum to inspire musicians.

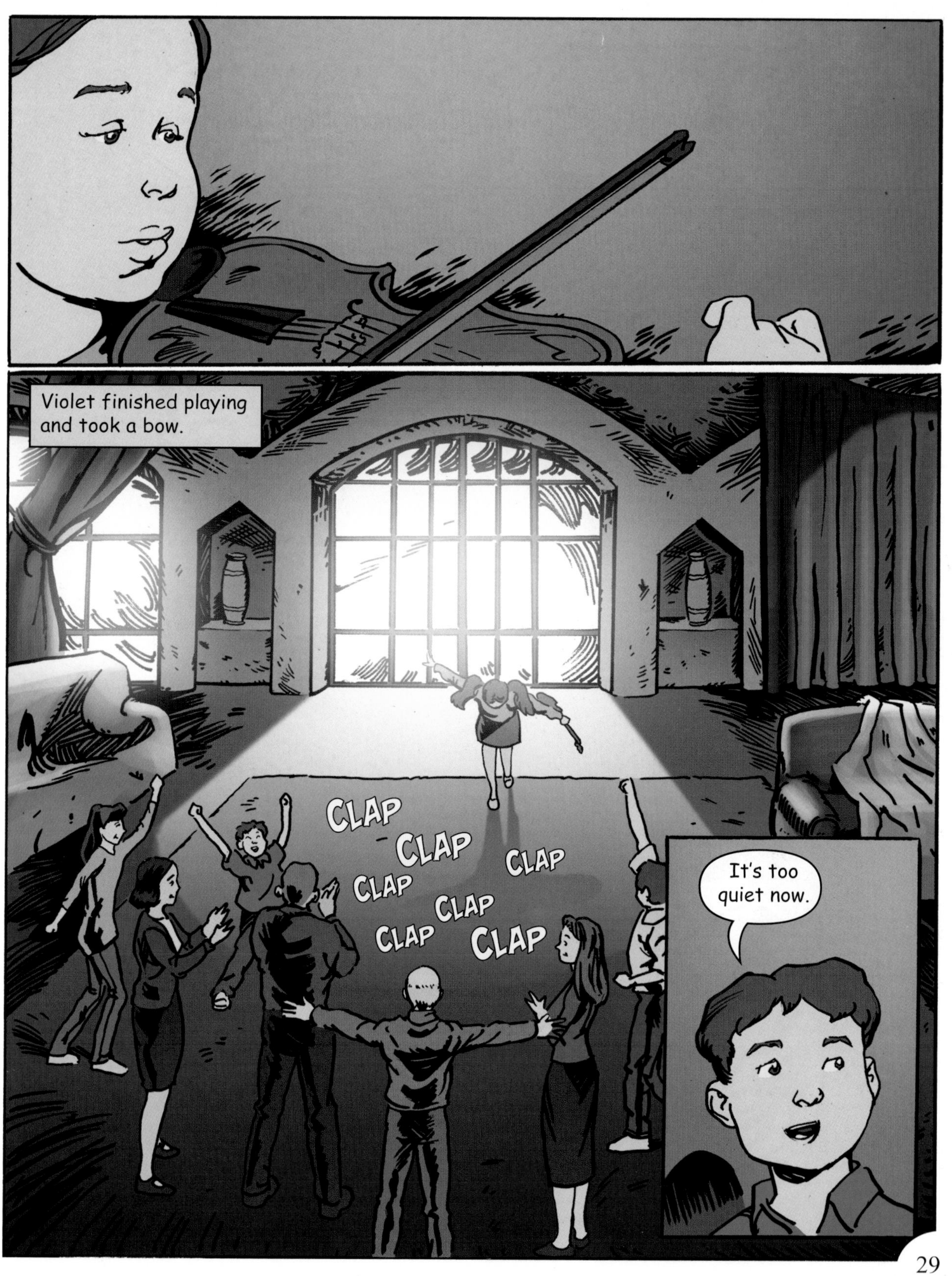
Violet finished playing and took a bow.
CLAP CLAP CLAP CLAP CLAP CLAP CLAP
It's too quiet now.

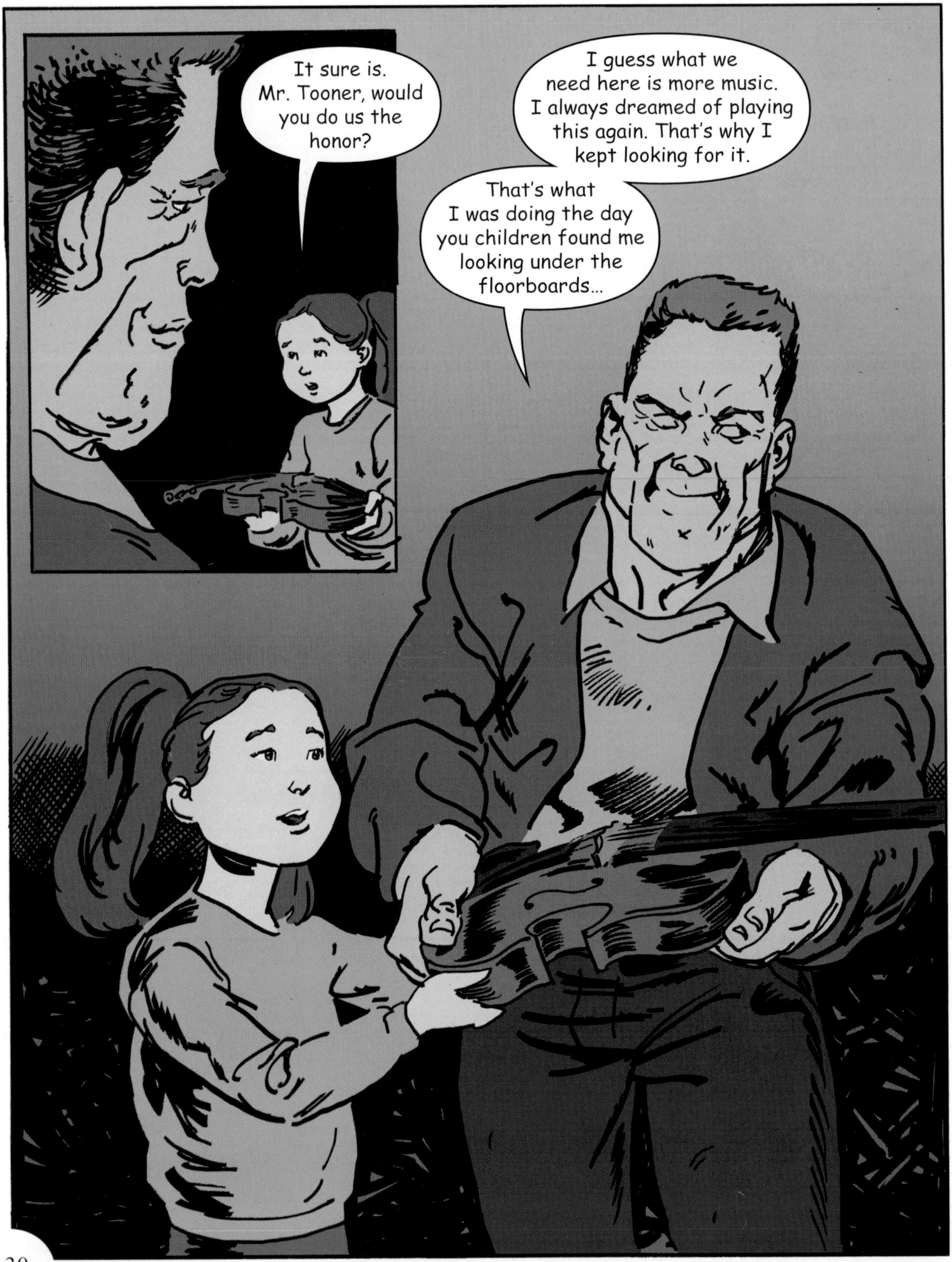
It sure is. Mr. Tooner, would you do us the honor?
I guess what we need here is more music. I always dreamed of playing this again. That's why I kept looking for it.
That's what I was doing the day you children found me looking under the floorboards...

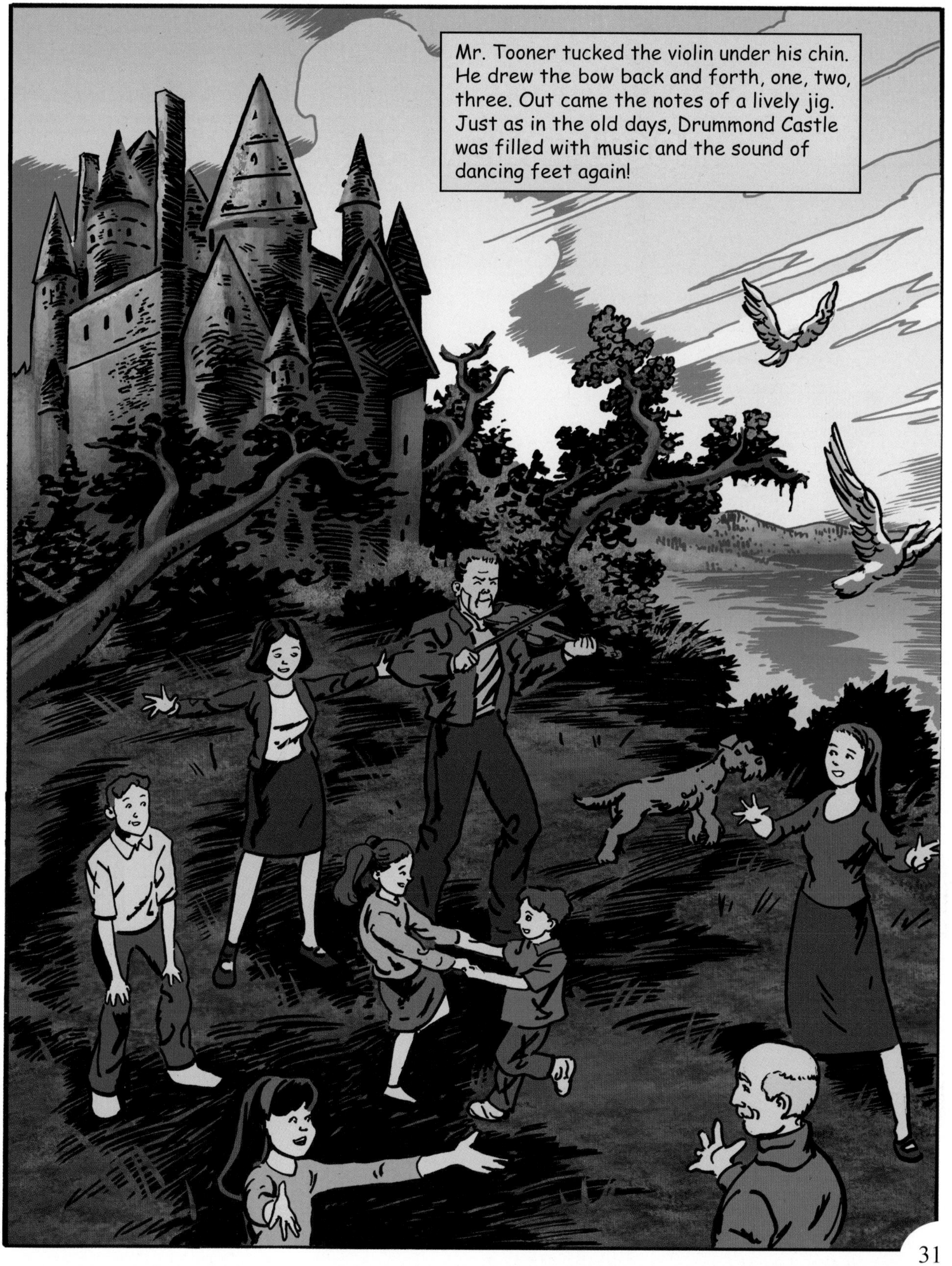
Mr. Tooner tucked the violin under his chin. He drew the bow back and forth, one, two, three. Out came the notes of a lively jig. Just as in the old days, Drummond Castle was filled with music and the sound of dancing feet again!

ABOUT THE CREATOR

Gertrude Chandler Warner was born on April 16, 1890, in Putnam, Connecticut. In 1918, Warner began teaching at Israel Putnam School. As a teacher, she discovered that many readers who liked an exciting story could not find books that were both easy and fun to read. She decided to try to meet this need. In 1942, *The Boxcar Children* was published for these readers.

Warner drew on her own experience to write *The Boxcar Children*. As a child she spent hours watching trains go by on the tracks near her family home. She often dreamed about what it would be like to live in a caboose or freight car—just as the Alden children do.

When readers asked for more Alden adventures, Warner began additional stories. While the mystery element is central to each of the books, she never thought of them as strictly juvenile mysteries. She liked to stress the Aldens' independence. Henry, Jessie, Violet, and Benny go about most of their adventures with as little adult supervision as possible—something that delights young readers.

During her lifetime, Warner received hundreds of letters from fans as she continued the Aldens' adventures, writing nineteen Boxcar Children books in all. After her death in 1979, her publisher, Albert Whitman and Company, carried on Warner's vision. Today, the Boxcar Children series has more than 100 books.